"SPEED AND THE DISCIPLINES ARE USUALLY INCOMPATIBLE, COMMANDER," SPOCK SAID.

Now it was Ae̶̶̶̶̶̶̶̶̶̶̶̶̶̶̶̶̶̶̶̶. She was afraid, but she ̶̶̶̶̶̶̶̶̶̶̶̶̶̶̶̶̶̶̶̶̶̶̶̶̶̶e her actions. Her need, or rather the need of others, was too great.

Spock was very still. At last he turned back to her. "Commander," he said, "it is possible that you might be taught. There is one condition in which speed does not obtain as an issue."

She swallowed. "Mind-meld," Ael said.

A silence fell again.

"But there is a problem," said Ael.

"There are certain . . . ethical constraints," Spock said. "There are constraints against teaching the disciplines, any of them, to those who have not committed themselves to—"

"Surak's strictures for peace," Ael finished for him, softly, and smiled a rather ironic smile. "Always Surak comes between our peoples, at the end." She stood up, glancing once again at the S'harien that hung on the wall, and turned away. "Mr. Spock, I am sorry to have interrupted you to no purpose. Please excuse me."

She was moving to the door when he put out a hand and touched her arm. The sudden unexpectedness of it shocked Ael to the core: she stood as still as if she had been struck so.

The hand that Spock had raised now fell. "It has occurred to me," Spock said, very low, "more than once of late, that there may be more than one road to peace."

STAR TREK®: RIHANNSU
By Diane Duane

#1: *My Enemy, My Ally*
#2: *The Romulan Way* (with Peter Morwood)
#3: *Swordhunt*
#4: *Honor Blade*

STAR TREK®

RIHANNSU

BOOK 4
HONOR BLADE

Diane Duane

POCKET BOOKS
New York   London   Toronto   Sydney   Singapore

An *Original* Publication of POCKET BOOKS

POCKET BOOKS, a division of Simon & Schuster, Inc.
1230 Avenue of the Americas, New York, NY 10020

A VIACOM COMPANY

This book is published by Pocket Books, a division of
Simon & Schuster, Inc., under exclusive license from
Paramount Pictures.

ISBN: 0-671-04210-6

First Pocket Books printing October 2000

10 9 8 7 6 5 4 3 2 1

POCKET and colophon are registered trademarks of
Simon & Schuster, Inc.

Printed in the U.S.A.

Editor's Note

In the days before *Star Trek: The Next Generation* came to the air and provided definitive information about the inhabitants of the Federation, their backgrounds and interactions, Pocket Books published several novels that speculated on the cultures and habits of alien species such as the Klingons and Romulans. Two of the most popular titles were *My Enemy, My Ally* and *The Romulan Way,* both of which focused on Romulan society. Although *The Next Generation* and its televised successors ultimately took Romulan culture in a different direction, fan interest in the Rihannsu, as Diane Duane described them, has remained strong throughout the years. This special series, which is meant to stand apart from established *Star Trek* continuity, continues the author's speculation on the intricate fabric of Romulan—or, rather, Rihannsu—society.

Chapter Six

SEMPACH WAS one of a newer, experimental class of cruisers, the *Constellation* class, named in memory of Matt Decker's old ship that had been lost against the planet killer in the L-374 system not so very long ago. The class-name ship and *Sempach* had been the first out of the shipyards, with *Speedwell* close behind, and all of them were already busy performing their basic function—trying out a new four-nacelle design that was supposed to provide starships with a more streamlined and reliable warp field, capable of higher speeds. The technology, referred to as "pre-transwarp" in some of the literature Jim had seen, was extremely interesting but technically somewhat difficult to understand, and Scotty had passed it on to his captain with a single comment: "Rubbish." Nonetheless, the technology seemed so far to be working all right, and the design crews had plainly been busy elsewhere too: the ship was very handsome from the outside, with a lean and rakish look to her. As the transporter effect wore off, Jim looked around *Sempach*'s transporter room, surprised at its size and its somewhat nonutilitarian look; there was even a small lounge area off to one side, with comfortable seating. *Kind of overdone,* Jim thought as he greeted the transporter technician at the console and then raised an eyebrow at himself. *She's affecting me. Still, it'd be nice not having to stand around waiting for visiting dignitaries to arrive.*

The transporter room doors opened, and Commodore Danilov came in, looking much as he had when Jim had last seen him in San Francisco: a brawny man of medium height, dark with a combination of Polynesian and eastern European blood, the dark hair going silver-shot now above a broad, round face, surprisingly unlined for someone of his age.

"Sir," Jim said, "you hardly had to come down here to meet me . . ."

The commodore gave him a wry look out of his sharp dark eyes as they shook hands. "Captain," Danilov said, "I'm still learning to find my way around this ship. I know I could have sent a lieutenant for you, but they get lost too. Come on."

They went off down the corridors together, the commodore making his way quickly enough despite his disclaimer. Jim's feelings about his superior officers ranged from the respectful to the occasionally scandalous, but here was one man in whose case he came down hard on the respectful side: twenty-five years in Starfleet, the kind of officer who flew a ship or a desk with equal skill—though he fought them more often than he simply flew them. Danilov's experience and effectiveness in battle had become legendary; in particular, he had probably scored more points during the last big war with the Klingons than any other commander except Captain Suvuk of *Intrepid,* until the Organians blew the whistle and stopped play. Jono Danilov had that invaluable commodity for a commander, a reputation for luck: he always seemed to come out only slightly scorched from any trouble he got into, no matter how the trouble seemed to seek him out—and it did.

"She's a fine ship," he said to Jim as they turned a corner, "a little fidgety at first, but she's settled in nicely now. Fleet's pleased: they're already flying the keels for the two new ones—*Stargazer* and *Hathaway.*"

Jim nodded. "She's a real lady, Commodore. And she still has that new-ship smell."

"I want to keep it that way for a while," Danilov said, shooting Jim a look, "and avoid getting things all scorched and smoky. The question is, will I be able to."

He came to a door without a label and waved it open. Danilov's quarters were considerably bigger than Jim's on *Enterprise,* and the office was also a lot more spacious. "Palatial," Jim said. "Rank hath its privileges."

"Hardly. This is the standard captain's cabin for

this model. Sit down, Jim, please. Can I offer you a brandy?"

"Thank you, Dan, yes."

He went over to a glass-doored cupboard and got it, and Jim sat looking around him for the moment at the furnishings, as spare as most field personnel's, but still individual: on the desk, a sleek, round old Inuit soapstone sculpture of a bear; a good amateur watercolor of the Ten-Thousand-Step Stair in misty weather, hanging on the wall behind the desk along with a brace of latoun-inlaid "snapdragon" flintlocks from Altair VI; a shaggy blue tree-pelt from Castaneda draped over the back and seat of the high-backed chair behind the desk.

Danilov handed Jim the drink in a heavy-bottomed crystal glass and seated himself. "*Viva,*" he said, lifting his glass.

"Cheers," Jim said, and sipped.

They sat appreciating the drinks for a few seconds, but no more. "So," Danilov said, "tell me about this little engagement you had here."

"Little!" Jim gave him a look. "Seven ships against two, sir; not my kind of odds. And circumstances were less than ideal."

"It would have been seven against one," Danilov said, "had things gone strictly by the book."

"They didn't," Jim said, "because I used some latitude in construing the orders that Fleet had specifically given me."

"Might I inquire about the reasons, Jim?" Danilov asked. "Or was it just on general principle?"

"I had a hunch."

Danilov let out a long breath. "No arguing with those," he said after a moment. "They've saved both our lives often enough before now."

"And it turns out to have been a good thing, in retrospect. It proves I was correct to be concerned about leaks of information from—" Even now Jim could hardly bring himself to say "Starfleet." "From Earth."

Dan sat back and looked at him. "No one but Fleet should have known where *Bloodwing* was going to be, or when," Jim said, "and regardless, there were seven Romulan vessels waiting for us there, cloaked. If Ael had been on site when originally scheduled, she would be dead now."

"Not a captive?"

"I doubt it. No one offered us the opportunity to surrender her. They just attacked."

"Your presence there might have affected their plans."

"That's occurred to me. But it doesn't matter, Dan. *Bloodwing*'s commander wouldn't have allowed herself to be taken alive. She would have fought until her ship was destroyed to prevent the Sword, or herself, falling into their hands."

"You're sure of that?"

"Yes."

"You're sure," Danilov said, looking steadily at Jim, "that your thinking on this particular subject is clear?"

"Dan," Jim said, nettled, " 'this particular subject' is a non-subject. My 'thinking' as regards Commander t'Rllaillieu is clear enough for my first officer,

5

who is something of an expert on the clarity of thought, and my CMO, who is something of an expert on humans in general, and me in particular." Danilov's gaze dropped. "The commander is a courageous and sometimes brilliant officer who, at the cost of her own career, sought us out and gave us valuable information which kept the balance of power from being irreparably destroyed. If the effectiveness of that intervention has been rendered short-lived by subsequent events, well, such things happen. If one of *us* had done the things she's done, he or she would have been loaded down with enough decorations to make the wearer fall face forward on trying to stand. But because she's from an unfriendly power, no one seems willing to take what she's done at face value."

There was a short silence. "The point is," Danilov said, "she's a Romulan. And Romulans plot."

Jim got up and started to pace. "Dan, with all due respect, you know as well as I do why you were so glad to get away from that desk in San Francisco. Politics! Romulans have politics just as we do, though possibly in a more complex mode. But this time, politics is failing, as it sometimes does, to keep this culture's internal conflicts from erupting into a war that affects others outside it. Including us. And we still have a problem at our end, because somehow very detailed information about our reactions to this situation is leaking out of Starfleet and getting to the Romulans—going straight to where it can do the most harm." Jim paused and gripped the back of his chair, leaning on it. "Something has to be done, and fast. Otherwise, when hostilities do break out, we're going to be in serious trouble."

Danilov sat back. "Your concern," he said, "is noted and logged."

"Which reassures me. But what's being *done* about it?"

Danilov just looked at him for a moment. "Jim, I can't discuss it."

Which meant he either knew something was being done, or knew that nothing was. "It's going to impair our conduct of this operation," Jim said, "if our personnel can't be sure that details of where they'll be aren't being piped straight through to the people who're going to be shooting at them."

"You leave the conduct of the operation with me," Danilov said, "since that's where Starfleet has placed it." The look he gave Jim implied that even enduring comradeship would not be allowed to interfere with some things.

Jim let the pause stretch out. "Yes, sir."

Danilov let out a long breath and reached out to pick up the smooth gray soapstone bear, turning it over in his hands. "Aside from that for the moment, Jim, message traffic has become an issue. It's way, way up on the Romulan side. We don't even need to be able to read those messages to know that a massive mobilization is under way, and to understand perfectly well where it's pointing."

"Lieutenant Uhura tells me that Starfleet message

traffic has also been reaching unusual levels," Jim said, sitting down again.

Danilov nodded. "Yes. With that in mind, we're carrying some material for you that Starfleet didn't want to send out through the ether. Strategy briefings, general intelligence from inside the Imperium . . . other information."

"They *are* afraid that some of our codes have been broken."

Danilov put the bear back down on his desk. "Yes. Some have been allowed to go 'stale' on purpose, for use when we *want* traffic to be intercepted. We've hand carried in two new encryption systems for you; all the rest of the ships in the task force have them already. You're to have your science officer install them immediately. One of them is for use now, the other is to be held."

"For when war breaks out . . ." Jim said.

Danilov looked at Jim with great unease. "No one in Fleet is saying that word out loud," he said. "But you don't have to be a telepath to hear people thinking it."

"And another thing about message traffic," Jim said. "Are you sure the monitoring stations are functioning properly? Those Romulan ships shouldn't have been able to cross the Zone, cloaked or not, without being detected by the monitoring web. Are some of those satellites malfunctioning? Have they been sabotaged? Or have the Romulans come up with a cloaking device that not even the monitoring stations' hardware can detect?"

Danilov frowned, shook his head. "It's being looked into, Jim. We're carrying a specialist communications team that will be performing advanced remote sensing and diagnostic routines to see what the story is when we get close enough to the Zone. For the moment, we're treating the information as reliable once it's been corroborated by other intelligence sources."

Jim nodded. He took out the data solid he had brought with him and passed it across the desk to the commodore, who put it on the reading pad. A little holographic text window leaped into being, scrolling down some of the contents with a soft chirring sound.

"While we're on the subject of things better not pumped into the ether at the moment," Jim said, "on this solid is our most recent work on the Sunseed project, including a way to tune starships' shields in order to screen out the worst of the artificial ion storm effect. I think this should be passed immediately to every other Starfleet vessel within range . . . and the preferred method of passing it should be by hand carry rather than broadcast."

Danilov looked at the text a moment longer, then nodded and touched the reading plate. The "window" disappeared with a chirp. "We'll pass it to them tomorrow," he said, turning the solid over in his hands.

"More material should be forthcoming shortly," Jim said. "But this kept our rear ends out of the sling at 15 Tri. Please make sure everyone takes it seriously."

"All right." Danilov looked up again. "There's no doubt that your forethought pulled this one out of the fire, Jim. It was a nasty situation, elegantly handled. But I should warn you, there'll still be some at Fleet who construe this kind of order juggling as an indication of someone trying to see how much he can get away with . . ."

"You're saying," Jim said, "that they're looking for proof of loyalty via blind obedience. Not the best place to look for it, Dan. But even if they *are* presently wasting their time worrying about minor issues like that, I don't think they'll have leisure for it much longer."

"No," Danilov said, "not once things get started tomorrow morning." He brought his standard desk viewer around toward him and glanced at it. "The first nonofficial meeting happens tomorrow morning. *Lake Champlain* and *Hemalat* have gone ahead to meet the Romulans and bring them in to RV Tri; we expect to hear that they've made contact in a few hours. Tomorrow afternoon, our ships' time, we'll be arriving at the rendezvous point. That evening, we have a social event to allow for some early assessments and to let both sides synchronize the meeting schedule—no one wants to be up in the middle of their own night while the other side is fresh. And then the main session gets under way, and we find out how much trouble we're really in."

"While behind us, on both sides, the eagles gather . . ." Jim frowned. "A lot of chances for things to go wrong, Dan. Somebody on one side or the other jumps the gun, and the shooting starts . . ."

"If any of my commanders do any such thing," Danilov said, "I will have their hides for hangings."

"A pity you can't enforce something similar on the Romulans," Jim said.

"We will play by the rules," Danilov said. "What the Romulans will do, the event will show."

Jim's smile was both grim and amused. "That's almost exactly what Ael said . . . You should come over and meet her this evening."

"I will," said Danilov, "once we're under way. I wouldn't mind getting out of this general area, just in case anyone else turns up."

"That's another concern, Dan. On that solid I gave you there's a 3-D analysis I did earlier. Later on you should take a look at it—"

"Why not now?" Danilov said. He put the solid down on the reader plate again and touched another control. Jim's hologram of the area where Empire, Imperium, and Federation all met now sprang into life in the air.

Jim's smile was annoyed. "Dan, it's just not fair that you have all these slick new gadgets when I—"

"Now, now," Danilov said, "thou shalt not covet thy neighbor's ship."

"Yes, well. But my neighbor's weaponry," Jim said, "is another matter."

Danilov smiled at that as he rotated the hologram. "Yes, *Sempach is* loaded for bear, isn't she? I've been wishing for a chance to use what she's got. Now I wish I didn't have to . . . and I'm becoming increasingly sure I will."

He paused, looking at the hologram. "You think there might be a multiple-location breakout."

"It's occurred to me."

"Fleet's been thinking that way too." Danilov looked at the hologram, sighed, and reached sideways to pick up his bear again, turning it over and over in his hands. "And there sit the Klingons. Or rather, they haven't been sitting; they've been running amok in the Romulan fringe systems—smash-and-grab stuff, asset-stripping the furthest planets."

"Suggesting they know the Romulans are going to make a big move now and won't bother defending targets that distance makes difficult to support."

"It does suggest that, doesn't it," Danilov said. "Hints and suggestions . . . I'd give a lot for some recent hard data from a source I trust."

"You may get some of that shortly."

"I desperately hope so." He turned away from the hologram and put the bear aside. "Well, is there anything else?"

Jim and the commodore looked at each other somewhat somberly as Jim stood up. "As regards Starfleet's concerns about me," Jim said, "you don't believe them, Dan, do you? You know me better than that."

Danilov didn't say anything for a long moment. "Look, Jim," he said finally, "people change. We're scattered all over the galaxy, all of us, for prolonged periods of time, in strange and sometimes disturbing circumstances. Starship captains are selected for stability, we both know that. But there's a galaxy full of unknowns out there, not to mention the ones at the bottom of the human mind . . . and things that can't always be predicted do happen. In a ship of this class, it's hard to avoid thinking frequently of Matt Decker."

"Matt was a one-off."

"Garth of Izar."

"That wasn't his fault. The alien treatment that saved his life—"

"Ron Tracey."

Jim grimaced.

"Jim," Danilov said, "we may or may not be a breed apart, but when starship commanders go off the rails, we do it spectacularly. Now, don't mistake me. I know perfectly well you're not likely to do anything like what Matt did. But every heart has its weaknesses, and conflicting loyalties can crucify a man faster than anything else."

"You can tell the fleet admiral," Jim said, standing very straight, "that my loyalties to the Federation and to Starfleet are quite clear, in accordance with my oaths to both those organizations. Starfleet Command should relieve me immediately if they think otherwise. But I will fight such a course of action, for they have *no* evidence whatsoever to back up any such suspicions. And I will win that fight."

Danilov looked at him steadily. "They sent you ahead to warn me, didn't they?" Jim said.

"I volunteered to make this side trip when I saw which way the wind was blowing back on Earth," Danilov said after a moment. "We've known each other a good while, Jim. You were the most ornery.

ensign a first-time lieutenant ever had to keep in order. But you wouldn't lie to a shipmate then, and I don't believe you'd lie to a fellow officer now. Indeed, you weren't all that good at lying when you had to."

"Possibly the root of this whole problem," Jim said softly, remembering how he had flinched, long ago, at reading the sealed orders from Starfleet that finally sent *Enterprise* into the Neutral Zone under the command of a captain who had to seem to be losing his marbles. *And as for this time . . .*

"Yes. You know the truth, and I'm sure you're telling it to me. But, Jim, you understand . . . *they* have to be sure."

"I understand," Jim said. "But it doesn't make me any happier about it, at a time like this, to find them so damned uncertain."

"No one promised us these jobs were necessarily going to make us happy all the time," Commodore Danilov said. "And our superiors are as mortal as we are, and as fallible."

"They are?" Jim said. "There go all my illusions."

Danilov chuckled. "Jim, our three ships will leave immediately for the task force rendezvous point at RV Tri. *Nimrod* will join us in a couple of hours, and *Ortisei* shortly thereafter. We should find *Hemalat* and *Lake Champlain* waiting for us with the Romulans: *Speedwell* has another errand and may arrive a little late. A little before we arrive at RV Tri, *Ortisei* will escort *Bloodwing* out of the area. Together they'll stay some light-years out of detection range until and unless they're called in."

"I'll pass that on to Commander t'Rllaillieu," Jim said.

"Will she cooperate?" Danilov said, looking closely at him again.

"She will," Jim said. "But I must tell you that she's already made it plain she has no intention of freely giving herself up to the Romulans if they ask for her."

"That could be a problem."

"It has to be one that Starfleet's anticipated. And it's a problem only if they decide they want to hand her over to the Romulans. Which, taking that into account"—he nodded at the hologram hanging in the air, burning in red, blue, and green—"isn't going to keep them from going to war now. Not after what they did at 15 Tri."

Danilov looked at the hologram. "I wish I could be sure," he said. "The Federation isn't. Part of our job here is to find out whether this war really has to happen."

"You may find out the answer," Jim said, "by being in the first battle, Dan."

"We're prepared for that," Danilov said. "But just as prepared to walk away, if there's any way to have peace break out instead."

"Amen," Jim said, reaching down to the desk and lifting his glass.

They knocked their glasses together and tossed off the remainder of the brandy. Jim put his glass down as Danilov did. "Jim," Danilov said. "I know what

shape of orders they cut you. Please . . . be careful . . .
because you're being closely watched."

By you, old friend, Jim thought. "Thanks for the
warning," he said as Danilov stood. "No, it's all
right, Dan. I can find my way out."

Danilov sat down again, throwing him an amused
look. "Later, Jim."

He left Danilov there looking at the holographic
representation of the Triangulum spaces, and only got
lost once on his way back to the transporter room.

Rihannsu song spoke wistfully enough of the ancient morning and evening stars, the old ships, long
fallen from orbit. *Nowadays, though,* Teleb tr'Sathe
thought, *we have only the one . . . but it's better by
far.* Often enough, when on leave on ch'Rihan, he
had looked up from some balmy beach or forest path
and tracked it across the night sky. Right now he
could not see it, but that was only natural: he was in
it. *But not for long!*

Teleb turned from the wide plasteel port looking
down on ch'Rihan and gazed back across the loading bay. It was a space half a *stai* wide, one of
twenty docking and loading facilities arranged
around a vast spherical central core that was big
enough to take even the largest of Grand Fleet's starships. Ur-Metheisn was probably one of the biggest
orbital ship-servicing facilities anywhere in known
space; even the Klingons and the Federation had
nothing to match it. They preferred smaller facilities,
more spread out among their colonies. The Rihannsu

school of thought preferred larger central facilities, "hubs," and this was the first and greatest of them: Sunside Station, the undisputed ruler of the skies over ch'Rihan. From it all the defense satellites were controlled and coordinated; from it the Fleet's ships were dispatched all over the Empire, executing the decisions made by the great-and-good down in the Dome. This was the beating heart of the Grand Fleet, and the kindly Elements had seen fit to drop Teleb right into the middle of it, his captain-apprenticeship successfully passed and himself newly promoted, the pins now bright on his collar, with his own cruiser *Calaf* poised graceful and nearly ready to go outside the docking and loading tube, and the prospect of battle in the offing. Life could not have looked brighter to him if Teleb had stared straight at the sun.

For the moment, he was doing what his mentor-captain had advised him—standing by and letting his crew get on with their jobs—though he would have much preferred to be right in the middle of them, hustling the loading crew, watching every detail. The excitement was definitely getting the better of him now. *Artaleirh!* When Teleb had seen the orders, he had nearly begun to sing with the sheer excitement of it all. Artaleirh was a vital system, and the news of the rebellion there had shocked and horrified him. But there would not be a rebellion for much longer. The sight of six cruisers in their skies would shortly remind those people of their proper loyalties. *But if it doesn't*—Teleb frowned. He didn't much care for the idea of having to make war on other Rihannsu. Weren't there Klingons and Feds enough to destroy? But there was no place for rebellion if the Empire was to remain strong in the face of her enemies elsewhere in the galaxy. *I am the servant of the Senate and the Praetorate,* he thought. *I am the strong arm of the Empire. I am a captain in Grand Fleet, and I will carry out my orders and win victory over the Empire's enemies, within it or without it, at whatever cost!*

Then Teleb grinned. "Adolescent effusions." That was what his mentor-captain Mirrstul had called such statements, though she had been kindly enough about it. Well, she had a right to her opinions: she was a doughty warrior and a brilliant tactician. But he could not imagine her ever having been young. As for himself, while he had his youth, he was not going to waste it on too much somberness.

Teleb leaned against the bulkhead with his arms folded, watching one of the specialist loading crews bringing in the last batch of photon torpedoes, trundling them quickly down the huge loading tube into *Calaf*'s lower weapons bay. He glanced at the chrono woven into his uniform sleeve. *Almost ready,* he thought. Teleb wanted very much to be the first to have the honor of reporting his ship ready to take off on this mission. *A few breaths more, then I will take my bridge and be the first to make the announcement—*

Then he caught sight of a tall dark shape walking quickly across the floor of the vast bay toward him, and he smiled slightly. Full dress uniform, glittering in black-gold and black; on departure day, you would never see Jisit in anything else. She was trying hard to look sober and serious, as befitted one setting out on an important mission, but such a demeanor always sat oddly on her as far as Teleb was concerned. His memory always overlaid them with the image of Jisit as she had been on that outrageous party night after her return from her first campaign, completely sozzled on ale, wearing a strange pointed hat with a tassel and singing "The High Queen's Bastard Daughter" to her crew and his in a key yet to be discovered by any other sentient being.

"Well, Captain tr'Sathe," she said, coming up to him and giving him two breaths' worth of bow.

"Well, Captain t'Nennien," he said, and gave it right back to her, to the very fraction of a second.

Then they both burst out laughing and collapsed into one another's arms. "Are you excited?" she hissed into his ear. "I can't bear it. I think I'll scream."

"Don't. They'll think you're singing again."

She laughed even harder and held him away. "Beast!"

"Guilty," Teleb said. "Is *Teverresh* ready?"

"Two loads to go yet, and my master engineer is complaining about retuning the warp drive before we leave. You'll beat me again, you fiddly little *neirrh.*"

He grinned. "I must keep you in your place somehow."

"Oh, and what would that be?"

"Behind me."

"Behind your back, you mean." The grin went a little more sober. "But that way, with me and *Teverresh* there, maybe no one will stab you in it. It's not a safe place we're going, Teleb. Artaleirh has gone quiet."

"Oh?"

She shook her head. "The time limit on the ultimatum expired two hours ago. They made no answer to the Senate's last warning. We will have to implement our orders to the full."

Teleb sighed. "Are they all gone mad? With the Klingons running about savaging everything they can, this is no time to renounce the Empire's protection."

"Mad or not, we will call them back to their proper loyalty," Jisit said, ". . . or relieve them of it and take it on ourselves."

"And win glory . . ."

"I don't know about the glory," Jisit said, "but we'll carry out our orders, make our frontiers safe, and uphold the rule of law. That's good enough for me. Maybe pick up a few points toward my next promotion." She poked him none too gently in the shoulder. "And as for you, *you* stay out of trouble when we get there. It would be embarrassing for me to have to save you again, now that they've finally trusted you with *Calaf* without old Mirrstul looking over your shoulder."

"What do you mean, save me *again?*" But Teleb's chrono chirped softly. "That's it," he said, glancing over at the loading tubes. The Sunside-based loading crews were leaving, pushing the last of the floater pallets in front of them. "I should go."

"Go on," Jisit said, "and I'll resume reminding you of the Elements' own truth, which you are pleased to refuse to see, after this operation's over. Mind your crew now, Captain!"

"You mind yours, Captain," he said. She turned, but he caught her by the hand and she paused. He bowed over that hand, low enough to breathe softly on the back of it.

She smiled, gripped the hand as he straightened. "Message me tonight, after we make warp."

"I will."

She turned and headed away across the loading bay, and Teleb hurried across to *Calaf*'s loading tube to make one final check on the condition of the weapons hold before going up to his bridge. He was humming the first line of "The High Queen's Bastard Daughter" as he went up the tube ramp into *Calaf*'s belly, and away to his first real war.

Jim was still thinking about *Sempach*'s weapons when he got back. The thought led to the idea that he'd like to look over her warp engines at some point, and that thought reminded him of something else. He paused in the corridor and hit a comm button. "Bridge."

"Bridge. Chekov here."

"Mr. Chekov, is Mr. Spock on the bridge?"

"He is on a scheduled break, Captain. I believe he has gone down to the main mess."

"Very well," Jim said. "Coordinate with the helm officer on *Sempach;* then notify *Bloodwing* we're setting course for RV Trianguli and implementing immediately."

"Aye, aye, sir," Chekov's voice came back.

"Kirk out."

Jim headed off down the corridor, caught a turbo-lift, and made his way down to the mess. There he found not only Spock but also McCoy, both finishing their lunches at one of the tables nearest the wall, both reading from electronic clipboard-padds as they did. Spock glanced up. "Captain—" he said.

"Finish your lunch, Mr. Spock, there's no rush about anything." Jim went over to the hatch and got himself a chicken sandwich and a cup of coffee, then sat down with them.

"How was your meeting with the commodore?" McCoy said, pushing his clipboard away.

Jim made a rather wry face. "Affable enough. But Fleet is antsy, as I expected, about our association with *Bloodwing* . . . even though they suggested we renew it. Suspicions rear their ugly heads." He sighed, shook his head, and bit into his sandwich.

McCoy snorted. "Invisible cat syndrome."

It took a moment of dealing with the sandwich before Jim could respond. "What?"

"As regards the commander, anyway."

Spock glanced over at McCoy. "If I remember correctly, the paradigm was first used by a religious apologist on Earth in the early twentieth century."

"That's right. Say somebody comes along,"

McCoy said, "and points at a chair and says to you, 'There's an invisible cat in that chair.' Now, *you* know the person's nuts. You say to them, 'But there's nothing there. The chair's empty.' Their response is, 'And isn't that exactly how it *would* look if there were an invisible cat in the chair? See, you've proved my point.' "

"Argumentum ex fallacio," Spock said.

"In your case, Jim—" McCoy had the grace to look just slightly abashed. "Well, come on. The source of all this trouble is that your opposite number's female. Bearing in mind some of your past behavior—not that I'm casting any aspersions, mind you—what *are* they supposed to think?"

Jim made a wry face. "This is just another way of saying it's all my own fault, isn't it?"

Spock addressed himself with renewed interest to his salad. "Jim," McCoy said, "they'll think what they think. You're not going to be able to change it, so you may as well just get on with what you were going to do anyway. How was the rest of your meeting?"

"Troubling," Jim said. He paused as a group of six or seven crewmen came into the mess and took a table, then headed for the food dispensers. "I think they're expecting the balloon to go up with a bang sometime after the talks with the Romulans, but no one seems to be clear about just when, or what will trigger it."

"I bet half of them are just hoping it doesn't happen, somehow," Bones said. "That the Romulans will just back down."

23

That thought had occurred to Jim, and it was making him nervous. He drank some coffee. "This time, I think that would be a serious miscalculation," he said. "Spock, I know perfectly well we run frequent readiness checks on all the weapons systems and the engines, but I want Scotty to use this next day or so to go over absolutely everything defense-oriented with a fine-tooth comb. Tell him to co-opt as much assistance from less busy departments aboard ship as he feels he needs to make sure that everything—*everything*—is in working order."

"Yes, Captain."

Jim finished his coffee and put the cup aside. "We also have some new cryptographic equipment or routines, or both, to be installed in the comm system and the main computer; they'll be coming over from *Sempach*. Which reminds me. Those automations Ael wanted you to have a look at? You never did report on those."

"It was not a very pressing matter, Captain. I wrote you a report, which you may not yet have seen."

Jim did his best to look unconcerned, but he knew he had been letting his paperwork slip a little lately. "Um. Well, what's the verdict?"

Spock put aside his empty bowl of salad and steepled his fingers. "I was able to assist them in several areas where newer programming and hardware needed to be restructured to interleave correctly with other, older control programs and routines," Spock said. "*Bloodwing*'s personnel have been most ingenious, and I should also say innovative, in compensating for their present lack of manpower. But here and there conflicts had occurred, since some of the newer programming was done by crewmen with less expertise than might have been desired, and the automation reprogramming had extended to almost every system aboard the ship."

"Almost?"

"There was one notable exception," Spock said. "The ship's engines did not appear on the list of augmented systems which I was asked to examine."

Jim thought about that for a moment. "Well, they didn't lose too many people from their engineering department during the trouble, as I remember. And tr'Keirianh is a fairly hands-on sort, from what I can make of him. Maybe he's uneasy about allowing such a crucial system to be automated."

"It could be, Captain," Spock said. "It could also be that there was something involving *Bloodwing*'s engine systems that the commander or the master engineer did not care to have me see."

Jim took another swig of coffee, considering that briefly. "Any evidence to support such a conjecture?"

"Little, and that circumstantial," Spock said. "Should another opportunity arise to investigate this, however, I confess I might attempt to do so."

"Curiosity, Mr. Spock?" Jim said.

Spock raised an eyebrow.

"Well, never mind it for now," Jim said. "Though if the opportunity arises this evening to do a little discreet inquiry, feel free." He sighed. "I won't be down in rec for long: I've got to start getting caught up on my paperwork. Meanwhile, when Ael and her people come by this evening to meet the commodore, see to it that each of them has an escort permanently within eyeshot. Security is going to become more of an issue now."

"I will see to it, Captain," Spock said. "Have you any preferences as to who should be assigned to the commander?"

Jim considered for a moment. "Now that you mention it . . ."

The darkness of the caverns, when the lights were turned down to their lowest, often seemed to amplify every sound, every breath. So it seemed very loud to Mheven when her mother spoke up suddenly out of what ought to have been her sleep.

"I hear," said Rrolsh. "I'm going out."

Mheven was at first not sure she hadn't been dreaming the words, for she had been thinking them, on and off, for nearly the past twenty days, since she came back from a mission. *Is it really that long,* she thought, *that we have been down in this darkness? It seems like a thousand years.* The sun—she dreamed about that too, golden in an emerald sky, but she knew she was not going to see it anytime soon. Up there, in the light and the air, more light than just the sun's was raining down on the fertile land. The sky was still filled with ships raining down fire. The crops were all surely burned now, the forest blanket-

ing these hills all charred, if what had happened to
the city had been any indication.

"Mother," Mheven said to the unseen presence
across the room, "you're half asleep. You know
they've been scanning the surface constantly. Anyone who goes out will be caught and interrogated,
and they'll discover where we are. Then all this will
be for nothing."

A faint sound of bedding being discarded drifted
across the darkness of the cavern. Mheven sighed
and fumbled for the little battery lamp.

At her touch it glowed up to its preset level—low;
no one down here wasted power. Since the destruction of the concealed solar arrays in the last spate of
bombing, there had been none to spare. Mheven
looked across the low-ceilinged little rest-cave and
saw what she expected: the water trickling down its
dank walls, the supplies of food and water and ma-
teriel stacked up in their crates at the back of the
cave, and the beautiful, drawn, tired, aging face of
her mother popping suddenly out of the cold-tunic
she was hurriedly pulling over her head. That grim
face looked at her; those eyes, fierce and eager,
looked into hers.

"You can't hear it?" she asked.

"Hear what?"

"I'm going out!"

Her mother scrambled up out of the bedroll and
headed for the sleeping cave's entrance, which had
someone's blanket hung up over it as a screen
against the lights always burning on the other side.

Mheven sighed and pulled on her own tunic. Kicking her bedroll aside, she went after her mother.

The main cavern, even with the tiny lights that were all the group now allowed itself, was still spectacularly beautiful. There had been a time when people had come from all over this part of the Empire to see these caverns, a natural wonder as astonishing in their way as the firefalls at Gal Gath'thonng on ch'Rihan; possibly the biggest natural caverns in all the Empire's worlds, but no one knew for sure, because no one had ever completely explored them in all the time the planet Ysail had been colonized, a matter of several hundred years. The caverns stretched beneath the smaller of the planet's two continents, Saijja, from the cliffs of Eilmajen in the east nearly to Veweil in the west, and they were so deep and complex that they had never even been completely mapped. Scanners could not reach so deep, not even the powerful ones used from space.

The refugees had picked this spot for their labors because it was one of the deepest caverns and because it was unknown to outsiders. Though in more peaceful times tourists had constantly been passing through one part or another of the Saijja Caverns, there had always been parts of the cavern complex that no tourist had ever been shown: the spelunkers' secrets, the private delights of those inhabitants of the planet who made it their business to come here every chance they got in leisure time, exploring a frontier that was not infinite but that would certainly take thousands of years to discover fully.

This one, the greatest cavern to be found for several hundred miles in any direction, was called Bheirsenn: "bright in the night," in the local dialect. When the lights were on, it was bright indeed—a vast bubble of air trapped in the depths of the planet, roughly a mile and a half in diameter, ceilinged in terrifyingly huge and glittering stalactite chandeliers of limestone, calcite, and quartz crystal. That impossibly distant ceiling shone bright as a hazy sky when the great high-intensity lights were on. They were not on much lately, what with the power crisis, but even with the lights dimmed, the distant pendant crystalline stalactites glittered faintly like faraway galaxies, like the points of stars. It was a space difficult for even the most ground-shy Rihannsu to feel claustrophobic in, one of awe-inspiring beauty.

And it was also a perfect place for making weapons of all kinds, especially bombs. From the great main cavern, hundreds of smaller caves budded off in clusters and chains, a labyrinth that only those who lived there could ever master. Working separately, the technicians and the people whom they had trained occupied small, dense-walled stone rooms in which they could work with deadly explosives and other dangerous technologies without being concerned about triggering a cataclysm. The whole group, totaling about five hundred people, had been down here for almost a year now. They had slipped away with their families and even their pets when the government had declared Ysail to be a "primary resource world." Others, at a distance, might have been fooled about what this meant, but the Ysailsu knew all too well. The Empire had seized all the industry on their planet. Then, when there was bitter protest at this, they had sent ships from Grand Fleet, carrying troops from the Army and Intelligence, to round up the population of a couple of cities and send them off to work camps, expecting the rest to settle down and do as they were told.

It had not worked out that way, for over the centuries the Ysailsu had developed what the Empire considered an irrational attitude: they thought *they* owned their world. The small population of the planet rose in nearly simultaneous rebellion. Immediately after that, the Empire began bombing it—very selective bombing, of course, concentrating on the cities and taking care to do no harm to industrial resources. The Ysailsu, though, partaking in full of the legendary stubbornness of their parent species, had decided that if *they* could not profit from the industries they had spent hundreds of years building, then neither would the Empire. Led by a group of thoughtful and angry guerrillas, the Ysailsu took all the food, water, spare parts, power sources, and supplies of every kind that they could find, and went to ground in the caves en masse. They scattered themselves across the underside of their smaller continent, made themselves at home, and began blowing up their factories themselves.

All this, as well as the smoking cities and the ground shuddering with explosions, now seemed as distant to Mheven as a dream. The workers and fighters down here did not hear or feel the explosions. The caves were far too deep. There was no way the Empire could find them, and even if it did, no way it could reach them without dropping atomics on them, and since the Empire theoretically wanted to use the planet for something else later, even *they* would not have been that crazy.

Crazy . . . thought Mheven, concerned, watching her mother make her way into the dim light of the main cavern, heading for the little makeshift workspace where Ddoya had his "office." Ddoya tr'Shelhnae was as much of a leader as their group had: the one to whom everyone brought their problems, the one to whom the once-a-tenday gathering turned for suggestions and direction. He had been a doctor once, and he was one of the original group of guerrillas who had convinced the population to use the strength that the Element Earth had given them as they descended into it and sheltered in it. Earth—the quietest Element and maybe the most taken for granted, but possibly the most powerful. He had more than a little of that Element in his own makeup, Mheven thought. He was a quiet man, slow, thoughtful—but eloquent: as with the ground when it quaked, when Ddoya spoke, you paid attention.

Her mother headed across that big space toward him, where a little light shone in his workspace. Elements only knew when the man slept; Mheven sometimes suspected him of having a clone or two stashed in one of the caves. Now she could just make him out, small, burly, and dark, sitting in his workspace, bent over something, as she hurried along in her mother's wake. Various other people were up and around, heading here and there in the cave, about their business. They watched Mheven heading after Rrolsh, and even in the dimness she caught some smiles from them. Living here was like living in the bosom of a large and unavoidable family, or a small town. Everybody knew everything about everybody soon enough, and everybody knew that Rrolsh had something rare: the visionary gift, which sometimes made her a little strange.

Mheven blushed but kept on going after her mother and finally caught up with her at the "door" of the workspace, which was just another blanket, one of four thrown over a cubical pipe-metal framework. It was fastened up at the moment, and Ddoya looked up at the two of them from the round, silvery thing he was holding in his hand.

"This isn't your shift, as a rule," he said. "Is there some problem?"

Mheven blushed again.

"Ddoya," Rrolsh said, "I heard something. Something's going to happen."

"What?"

Rrolsh looked frustrated. "I don't know for certain," she said. "But it's imminent."

He raised his eyebrows. "I could wish," Ddoya said, "that our distant ancestors had left us some instructions about what to do with such talents as yours when they crop up, for I'm sure I don't know what questions to ask you to help you be more definite. Nonetheless, we'll go on alert, if you feel the need, Rrolsh. I haven't forgotten that last incident with the government courier."

Rrolsh sighed and shook her head, looking suddenly weary. "It's not that close," she said. "Or . . . it's not that serious. I can't tell which. I only caught a feeling, a word . . ."

"Well, let it rest for the moment," he said. He looked past her at Mheven. "Meanwhile," he said to her, "we have another attack group going out in a few days. We should send some of these with them for testing. But I'd like you and your people to double-check these first."

Mheven was one of the group's engineers. Once her forte had been medical machinery, which was how Ddoya had recruited her. Now she had acquired a rather more destructive specialty, and what he held intrigued her. She held out her hand, and Ddoya passed the object to her. It was a flattened ovoid of silvery metal, about the thickness of her hand.

"Implosion charge?" Mheven said, turning it over.

"Combined implosion-disruption," said Ddoya. "Remember the old 'dissolution' fields that the warships used to use?"

"The ones that would unravel a metal's crystalline structure."

"That's right. An overlooked technology, but surprisingly suitable to being packed down small, these days, with the new solid-phase circuitry. This one goes off in two stages. The dissolution field propagates first, and then the imploder collapses the deranged matter. One of these"—he took it back from her carefully—"will scoop out a spherical section from a building, or a bridge, or a ship, something like twenty *testai* in diameter." He smiled grimly.

"How many do we have?"

"Five so far."

"I want to go along," Mheven said.

"Check with Ussi," Ddoya said. "She's coordinating. Was there anything else?"

Mheven shook her head.

"No," her mother said. "Ddoya . . . thanks."

"Don't thank me. I know it's difficult for you, and you bear this burden, and work as hard as any of us, as well."

A few others, faces Mheven recognized but was too tired to greet, were drifting over. Mheven sketched a wave at them, linked her arm through her mother's, and started back toward their rest-cave.

"I embarrass you," said her mother.

"Not seriously."

"I wonder what it was like, in the old days," Rrolsh said, sounding wistful. "When there were Talents in the ships, and telepaths, people for whom seeing more than one world, hearing more than spoken voices, was normal."

"Maybe someday we'll find out again," Mheven said. Hope was good: any distraction, sometimes, was good for turning one's mind from the idea that one might be living in a cave making bombs only until something went wrong, everything was found out, and they were all hunted down and killed.

"Maybe someday the Empire will just give up and—"

Her mother stopped and stood still. Mheven turned to her, and in the dimness she could just see her lips move. Then Rrolsh let go of her and turned back the way they had come. She went straight back to Ddoya, who, with the two people to whom he was talking, looked up at her, surprised.

"I heard it clearly this time," her mother said. "I heard it! Just a whisper in the darkness. It said *lleiset.*"

The others looked at each other, not knowing what to say.

Freedom . . .

Ddoya turned the new charge over and over in his hands, then looked up at her.

A soft *queep* from a small console on the floor beside his chair brought all their heads around. Eyes widened. Ddoya, in particular, looked at the thing as if he expected the little square console to stand up and bite him in the leg.

"Ddoya," said one of the fighters standing nearby, a man named Terph, "they can't be here yet. It's too soon."

"It could be a trick," said Lais, the other.

Silence, and then another *queep*.

The five of them looked at one another. No more sound was forthcoming, for the sound was the one realtime noise made by the narrow-bandwidth subspace transmitter-receiver until it was instructed to play. The receiver did not produce output in realtime: it took a coded digital squawk no longer than a millisecond, decompressed it, decoded it, and played it on command, recording and sending outgoing messages the same way. It was how their group kept in touch with the hundreds of others scattered through the caves, and they did not overuse it for fear of detection.

Ddoya got off his chair, knelt down beside the transmitter-receiver. He touched its controls in a coded sequence, and the transmitter's decode lights went on.

"The ships are coming," whispered the voice from the narrow-bandwidth subspace transmitter. "Repeat, the ships are coming. This is a multiple sighting, multiple confirmed. Relief will be with you within ten standard days. Events to follow will most likely cause the Fleet to withdraw. Prepare to emerge in force. More details are packed with this squirt. Unpacking now."

Ddoya looked up at them his stolid face suddenly alight with excitement. For a few moments he was as speechless as the rest of them. "Well," he said finally. "We'd better get everyone together to discuss this in the morning. Meanwhile, let's get back to planning the next raid."

They smiled at one another, a little more fiercely than usual. Mheven looked over at her mother and smiled. "So you were right," she said. "We *are* going out. All of us. But meantime, let's get caught up on our sleep."

They walked off together. But this time, as they went, Mheven's heart was pounding. Enough of her people had died waiting for this day when it would start, when they would not be fighting alone. Enough of them had died trying to bring it about. She herself might yet die in these next few days. But all the same, she smiled. And as she and her mother slipped back into the darkness of their sleeping place, Mheven wasn't entirely sure she didn't hear the same whisper.

Freedom . . .

In the rec room that evening, Ael looked up out of the great windows at the stars pouring past and let out a small sad breath. The time when she might freely enjoy this spectacular view was swiftly coming to an end. *Soon enough,* she thought, *I will be staring into a tactical display again, concentrating on objects moving in space much more slowly, relatively speaking, than the stars. I should enjoy this while I can . . . as far as possible.*

She glanced around. All about her, various crewmen sat and chatted, or gamed, as usual. Off in a small conversation pit nearby, Scotty and tr'Keirianh and K's't'lk were conversing with energy, occasionally waving hands or jointed glittering limbs in gestures strangely reminiscent of those which young Khiy and Mr. Sulu had been using the other day. Lieutenant Uhura was leaning over the back of one of the settles that formed the back of the pit, asking K's't'lk something. The answer came back in a bright spill of music, but oddly, with no words that Ael could hear. Curious, Ael started strolling their way, and a discreet rumbling accompanied her, like a boulder trying to roll along without making too much of a racket.

Ael had to smile, though the smile was doubtless somewhat edged with irony for a perceptive viewer. "Mr. Naraht," Ael said, "this duty must be a trial for you. Doubtless there are many more interesting things for you to be doing."

"Not at all, Commander," the Horta said, shuffling his fringes about a little as he came up alongside her. "Everything here is interesting."

"Surely you are putting a brave face on it," Ael said.

"Madam," Naraht said, "if you've ever lived in the crust of a planet with nothing to do but eat rock, and nothing to do after that but listen to your ten thousand siblings eat rock, and then listen to them talking about *having* eaten rock—after a while, *anything* else is interesting." His translator module emitted that rough, gravelly sound that seemed to be laughter, and his fringe tendrils shivered. "And when you notice that weird creatures who *don't* eat rock, or even talk about it much, are wandering around the place, they and their affairs are likely to become, by comparison, very interesting indeed."

Ael raised her eyebrows at that. Amid some human and Rihannsu laughter, she saw Uhura straighten up and head off purposefully, as if in search of something. "Might you not be overstating the case, Lieutenant? Most of us think our ordinary home life is boring. And your people, Mr. Spock tells me, are a most intelligent and complex species—"

"Far be it from me to argue with Mr. Spock,"

Naraht said. "My mother would come down on me like a ton of ore if she found out. But, Commander, intelligence doesn't necessarily imply culture."

Ael chuckled. As they came up to the conversation pit, Ael leaned against the back of one of the higher-backed semicircular settles on one side, glancing down with slight affection at tr'Keirianh. He was oblivious, concentrating on something Scotty was saying to K's't'lk. ". . . downright heretical, lass," Scotty said, "in the merely physical sense rather than the physics one."

K's't'lk sighed a long, jangling sigh, like a set of wind chimes out of sorts. "The distinction is strictly artificial," she said. "Or rather, it's a perception problem. The law of general relationships says—" She started singing again, a very bright precise sequence of notes. When she finished, after about ten seconds, tr'Keirianh, sitting with his head tilted slightly to one side, said, "I believe I nearly heard it that time. Perhaps the difficulty is with the way our people handle tonalities. But I am no musician. I never had any interest in music when I was younger, and nowadays I have little time, though I admit the inclination is forming—"

"For what, Giellun?" Ael said.

Her master engineer looked up at her with some amusement. "The commander is teaching us the basic elements of Hamalki physics notation, *khre'Riov*," he said. "Or trying to."

" 'Tis an exchange program, Commander," Scotty said. "She'll teach us this, and we'll teach her poker."

"And Khiy and Aidoann and I will teach her *aithat*," tr'Keirianh said.

Ael shook her head. "Elements send we all have time for all this," she said, "but, Mr. Scott, of your courtesy, what in the worlds is 'poker'? The translator suggests an iron stick. But I think I have found one of its blind spots; I don't think you speak of such."

A slow grin began to spread over Mr. Scott's face. "Poker is a game," he said.

Giellun's expression became somewhat more wicked. "If I understand Mr. Scott's description correctly," he said, "it is, like *aithat,* a way of equalizing the distribution of the crew's pay throughout the ship."

"Ah, me," Ael said. "Given our current circumstances, perhaps this would be useful." Though she wondered, for *aithat,* a gambling game based on the careful calculation of odds and the distribution of counters and tiles of fixed value among the players, already served that purpose. "But it is not a strategy game then, like your *schhess.*"

"Not in the same way—"

"Oh, I'm sorry, Commander, am I interrupting something?" Uhura said from behind Ael.

Ael turned. "Not at all, Lieutenant," she said, and then blinked in surprise, for Uhura was carrying a ryill, a particularly handsome one, maybe a century or so old, to judge by the patina on the inlaid wood, and well-cared for. "Air's name, where did you come by such a fine instrument?"

"The lute is Mr. Spock's," Uhura said. "He lends it to me occasionally. I was hurting my throat trying to match some of these higher notes K's't'lk's been producing, and if I want to learn how to at least communicate date and time coordinates in Hamalki, I need to be able to produce the sounds some other way, for practice purposes anyway." She sat down in the pit next to K's't'lk and began tuning the ryill for the octave she wanted. "The physics I'm in no hurry about, but the syntax and structure of the language shouldn't be too far beyond me. K's't'lk, would you give me one more example of the one you did just before I left?"

K's't'lk emitted one short burst of sound, a chord, followed by a short phrase that seemed to be in a major key, about five seconds long. Uhura finished adjusting the ryill's drone control and then mimicked the phrase. The tone of the ryill was excellent. Ael suspected that her estimate of its age was correct, for it was using the relatively old form of solid-state audio inlays, which gave a warmer, more intimate sound to the bass "stringing."

"Very close," K's't'lk said. "Einstein might not understand it, but I do. Add a note a fourth above the high note in the drone."

Uhura played the sequence again. "There you are," K's't'lk said.

Scotty was shaking his head. "Lass, if they'd put $E=mc^2$ to me that way when I was young," he said, "no telling where I'd be now."

"In a first chair at the Mars Philharmonic, possibly," K's't'lk said, and laughed. "Not that we couldn't still have used you in that capacity on Hamal. Sometimes I think Bach was one of us who took a very wrong turn and got born on Earth by accident . . ."

"Did I miss the folk singing?" said a voice from behind Ael. She smiled and turned to see the captain there.

"We are folk," tr'Keirianh said, "but the Commander here has been doing most of the singing."

K's't'lk chortled again and then launched into a long syncopated phrase full of sudden leaps up and down a very oddly assembled chromatic scale. Ael glanced at tr'Keirianh, curious to see if he made anything of it; to her it sounded like someone dropping a box of broken glass. Uhura frowned and started repeating the phrase, more hesitantly than the last time. The captain raised his eyebrows. "Marsalis?"

"Hawking," K's't'lk said. "The equation for working out the rate of evaporation of black holes."

"I should know better than to ask," the captain said. "Commander, might I borrow you for a moment?"

She inclined her head to him, then raised a hand to tr'Keirianh and the others and stepped away. Behind her, K's't'lk was saying, "All right. Here's an easy one—"

"What was that?"

"The formula for Planck time."

"Can I have that again? I missed it . . ."

Ael walked back in the direction of the great windows with the captain. Mr. Naraht remained behind for the moment. Very quietly, the captain said, "I just wanted to let you know that I've had one more word with the commodore. Unfortunately, he's not willing to be swayed on this. Starfleet is very insistent that you be taken out of the area while negotiations are ongoing."

"Well, I suppose I can understand that," Ael said. "But of course it will not be *Enterprise* that accompanies us."

"No," Jim said, "of course not. *Ortisei* will go with you."

"Well," said Ael, "once again I show myself a prophetess, though in these circumstances it takes little accomplishment to manage it." She glanced up at the great windows again. "But I appreciate your effort on our behalf. We will, at least, be able to keep in touch in the usual fashion."

"I'm going to have to be careful about that," the captain said. "Communications to and from all our ships are likely to be carefully watched, I think, and clandestine messaging could be misunderstood."

Ael nodded.

"Either way, we'll see to it that very frequent reports of the meetings, and anything else germane, reach you every day. And one other thing. The Romulan group has now been met by the first two escort ships. We'll all be at the rendezvous point within five hours."

Ael nodded again. "I will remain here just a little while longer," she said, "and then head back to *Bloodwing*. There is still a great deal to make ready."

He nodded too, looking tired—more tired than she could remember seeing him since the two of them had been surrounded by the blood and phaser fire of Levaeri V. *He feels the weight of what is about to happen,* she thought, *and the fear, even as I do. I wish I could give him some assurance of how things will go, but that is not in my power. Any more than it is in his gift to give such assurances to me.*

"I have a ton of paperwork to deal with," the captain said, "and I've been getting behind. Bearing in mind what we're going to be going into, I'd better get it sorted out before things heat up." He looked up again, met her eyes. "Commander, should I not see you again before things start . . ."

She bowed to him, three breaths' worth, then straightened. "No long farewells as yet, Jim," she said, then had to smile. She had never quite got used to calling him that with a straight face.

The captain grinned at her, understanding. Then he departed, lifting a hand in casual salute to the commodore across the room. That man's eyes went from the captain to Ael, rested on her a moment, then turned away again to the windows and the view of the ships pacing *Enterprise* through the night. Ael looked at the commodore for a few seconds longer. He was a likable man, Ddan'ilof, but cautious, reserved, like one new to high command and still slightly nervous of its weight and pressures; also a man who, it was plain, did not trust her. Ael had caught one or two glimpses of him looking at her and the captain while they had been speaking, once or twice, earlier this evening—not being obvious about it, but watching them all the same, with a quiet, assessing look.

Her own crew had thrown her a few looks like that over the past couple of months. They hadn't voiced any suspicions, naturally, but the looks had been there. Even after everything *Bloodwing* had been through under her command, it still came hard for Rihannsu to trust aliens, and the closer they became, in some cases, the harder her crew seemed to find it to trust them. There was irony in it, for *Bloodwing* had suffered more from the treachery of other Rihannsu than from any alien. Command back on the Homeworlds, and various members of her own crew, had been blades enough in Ael's side, and in the sides of those aboard *Bloodwing* who had honored their oaths, held their *mnhei'sahe,* and served her until Levaeri V and past it, out into the darkness of uncertainty and homelessness. Now they were the crew of a ship without a fleet, and a commander without rank. *And yet they serve me,* she thought, *while wondering if they may still be further betrayed by their own.*

While I wonder if I may be so betrayed as well . . .

The heavy rumbling sound came up slowly behind her as Ael looked up at those big windows. The stars poured by, and far nearer than they, two of the three other starships presently accompanying *Enterprise* rode off her starboard, sleek and silent and dangerous-looking in the shifting starlight shimmering on their hulls. It was not as if *Enterprise* did not have the same general look, but to Ael, at least, she no longer *seemed* dangerous.

And that perception, she thought, *may eventually prove fallacious. Beware . . .*

The rumbling died back to a faint shuffle. From

across the room there was another bright spill of notes, scaling quickly upward into a kind of melodious crash, followed by Uhura's and tr'Keirianh's and Mr. Scott's laughter. *Time to go,* Ael thought, *while I am still in good cheer.* She glanced down. "Mr. Naraht," she said, "perhaps you would be good enough to accompany me down to the transporter room."

"My pleasure, madam."

She had to chuckle, for he actually said *llhei,* bypassing the translator installed in his voder pack. "Very strange it is," she said as they left together and headed for the cargo lifts at the end of the corridor, "to find the seeming essence of Earth so mutable. Do you study languages, then, as well as sciences?"

"It's all part of biomaths, Commander," the lieutenant said. "Life needs language to understand itself, and the more language, the better. The translator is a tool, but sometimes it's more fun to get straight down into the matrix of thought and wallow—even if it does taste strange at first." There was a pause. "As for stone being so immutable, what about magma, then?" No question: the voice was smiling. "That's one of the few things I miss. It's been an age since I had a swim."

Ael stared at him as they went. "In *lava?*"

"We had a swimming hole," Naraht said. "When we were big enough, our mother took us. Oh, that first dive into the fire . . ." As they paused outside the lift, Naraht shivered all over, and Ael realized with astonishment that the gesture was one of sheer delight. "How scared we all were. And how silly we were to be scared. It stung a little, but it was worth it."

She got into the turbolift, and Mr. Naraht, with some difficulty, shuffled in behind her. The doors shut. "Deck nine," she said, and off it went, obedient. "Lieutenant," Ael said, "I ask you to forgive me if I transgress. But your people are a wonder to me—as if you were an aspect of my own folk's way of looking at the universe, of one of the Elements, indeed, suddenly come real. And it makes me wonder: how do *your* people see that universe? Not the physical parts of it, I mean. What lies beneath?"

He shuffled around a little, turning, almost as if to look at her. "It's odd you should phrase it that way," Naraht said. " 'Beneath.' We know well enough what's at the heart of our planet—of most planets. The pressure, the heat and density. But what if that were an idiom for something else? A heat that scorches but doesn't burn—the pressure so great it becomes total, the whole weight of being pressing down, with yourself at the center of it, accepting it, thereby defining it, creating it, eternal. The inexpressible richness, the transcendent temperature, down there in the deepest places beneath and within, the depth that never ends, increasing, crushing us into reality—" He paused, as if to recover himself. The diffidence Ael was used to hearing in his voice had been missing. "I'm still learning the language for this," Naraht said then. "I may be learning it for hundreds of years, while I talk to other people, learning what they think . . . so I can better find out what I think. It's frightening, a little, like that first jump into the lava. Afterwards you wonder why you waited so long, but it's still hard to go where your fears take you. Or where they would, if you let them." He paused. "Sometimes I think that's why I came here," Naraht said, more quietly. "I was afraid of the emptiness—first the air, and then the dark above it: the places where almost nothing was solid. But I said to myself, 'I'll jump anyway . . .' "

Ael nodded. "I see," she said. And after a moment she said, "I was half afraid to come here once, too. But I had no choice."

"Only half?" Naraht said.

Ael chuckled at that. "Earth you are indeed," she said, "and as such you see through stone readily enough with time. This noble ship—how I regretted, once, walking its corridors while being unable to bring it home to the Imperium in triumph as a prize of war."

"But that changed," Naraht said.

"It did," Ael said. Not even to him, personified Element or not, would she say just how. But what she now valued most about the *Enterprise*—most paradoxically, with an eye to the ship's many past encounters with *Bloodwing*—was its sense of being a sort of haven of peace. Though of course there were parts of it she still found most uncomfortable to be in: sickbay, particularly, and—

Ael swallowed. "Stop," she said. The lift paused. "Destination?" it said.

"Madam?" Naraht said. "Is there a problem?"

Ael stood there, turning the idea over in her head

for a moment. To her horror, she could find no good reason to reject it. "Mr. Naraht," she said, "perhaps we might make one stop before we leave."

"Certainly, Commander."

"Deck five," Ael said.

Off the lift went again, and presently its doors opened. Having had the idea, now Ael stood there frozen for several seconds. Embarrassment, though, finally moved her. She got out, Naraht rumbling along behind her, and stood in the corridor for a moment to get her bearings; it had been a different lift she had used the last time. Then she walked down the corridor, her heart pounding, to the door she remembered all too well.

Naraht did not comment, simply shuffled himself up against the wall to wait. Ael touched the signal beside the door.

"Come," said the voice from inside.

She went inside; the door closed behind her.

Spock looked at her in considerable surprise and got up from the seat behind his desk, where he had been sitting with fingers steepled, gazing at something on the desk viewer that Ael could not see. "Commander," he said.

"Mr. Spock," Ael said, "I have interrupted you at meditation, I see. Please forgive me." She turned to go.

"There is no need," Spock said. "The meditation was not formal. How may I assist you?"

Ael opened her mouth, but could find nothing to say.

If this astonished her, she could only wonder what

Spock must think of it. He showed no sign of surprise, though, and merely pulled out a chair from the other side of the desk. "Please, Commander," he said, "sit down."

Ael sat in that chair, though it cost her some effort. She had sat in it once before, and the memory was still not scarred over sufficiently to touch without discomfort.

Her eyes slid up to the S'harien hanging on the wall, a curve of darkness all too like the one across the chair in her cabin, which she could feel looking at her, these days, more than ever. *There is your excuse,* her mind whispered to her. *Your last chance—*

"I have a problem, Mr. Spock," Ael said. "I have put off dealing with it for some time. It occurs to me that the most likely solution is unique, and that you possess it."

"A description of the problem would assist me," Spock said.

Ael swallowed again. "Starships," she said, "are not the only hardware my people have purchased from the Klingons of late."

"It would be only logical to assume as much," Spock said.

"Indeed. After Sunseed and the DNA acquisition project were stolen, there appeared a sudden enthusiasm for that piece of equipment known as the mind-sifter. It apparently has become very popular among the intelligence forces of the Two Worlds, for Rihannsu have no defense against it. And even though our own Fleet sees to it that those of us who command are given buried mental protections similar to your own command conditioning, even those would not suffice to protect us against the Klingon tool."

Spock nodded. "I believe your assessment is correct."

"One must plan for all eventualities," Ael said. "Worse may yet come to worst. Logic suggests that circumstance or accident might yet cause me to fall into their hands."

"I cannot deny that, Commander."

"Spock," Ael said, "I will be open with you. The stakes in this game have greatly increased since I first began to play. Where only my own life was involved, and those of *Bloodwing* who have sworn themselves to me with full knowledge of the continuing risk, I have been willing to depend on my own resources. But now many more people, well-intentioned but perhaps ill-informed of the dangers of aligning themselves with me, are becoming involved, and I must hold them in mind as well. I have no desire to betray those on the Hearthworlds and among the colonies whom I know are engaged in the struggle about to begin. Yet I may not be able to avoid doing so, if my enemies succeed in preventing me from ending my life before they do their will with me. Should this happen, those who would continue the fight after my death would have no chance to do so. My destruction would mean theirs as well, and that of their families and very likely even their acquaintances. Therefore . . ."

Spock waited.

"I would ask," Ael said, "whether there is among the mind disciplines one you might be able to teach me quickly, one that would allow me to make that end if other, more straightforward means are denied me. Or one that simply would make information I hold forever inaccessible to those who would use it against the ones who would continue the fight. I understand that this might be impossible . . ."

"Speed and the disciplines are usually incompatible, Commander," Spock said. "However . . ."

Now it was her turn to wait. She was afraid, but she would not allow fear to dictate her actions. Her need, or rather the need of those who looked to her to be protected from the Empire, was too great.

Spock was very still. At last he turned back to her. "Commander," he said, "it is possible that you might be taught. There is one condition in which speed does not obtain as an issue."

Ael swallowed. "Mind-meld," she said.

A silence fell again.

"I remember," Ael said, "the technique that you mentioned Captain Suvuk of *Intrepid* had used after being captured by the personnel at Levaeri V, to prevent my people extracting his command codes from him. *Kan-sorn.*"

"It could be taught," Spock said. "But there are other disciplines that might benefit you more, most specifically against interrogation. I have had some personal experience in this regard."

And then he was silent again.

"But there is a problem," said Ael.

"There are certain . . . ethical constraints," Spock said. "There are constraints against teaching the disciplines, any of them, to those who have not committed themselves to—"

"Surak's strictures for peace," Ael finished for him, softly, and smiled a rather ironic smile. "Always Surak comes between our peoples, at the end." She stood up, glancing once again at the S'harien that hung on the wall, and turned away. "Mr. Spock, I am sorry to have interrupted you to no purpose. Please excuse me."

She was moving toward the door when he put out a hand and touched her arm. The sudden unexpectedness of it shocked Ael to the core. She stood as still as if she had been struck so.

The hand that Spock had raised now fell. "It has occurred to me," Spock said, very low, "more than once, of late, that there may be more than one road to peace."

Ael looked up into that still, unrevealing face and thought she saw more revealed there than Spock intended. "If I err in my judgment," Spock said, "the price will be mine to pay, for a lifetime. Yet you too have paid a high price for your actions of late, yet have not regretted them."

"Imprecision, Mr. Spock," Ael said softly. "Bitterly indeed I have regretted my actions—some of them. Yet given the chance to repeat those actions, I would not do otherwise. Could not. *Mnhei'sahe* is its own reward—though sometimes that reward cuts deep. But what use is a sword that will not cut?"

It was Spock's turn now to glance up at the S'harien, then back at her. "I do not think I err," Spock said. "Commander, if you consent to this—"

She sat down again, trying to find calm. Spock slowly clasped his hands and stood still for a moment, the expression starting to go inturned; but his eyes were dark with concern, with final warning. "I must apologize to you in advance for any discomfort I cause you and for any lack of clarity in the transmission," he said. "I am not trained in the teaching of these techniques, though others have trained me in them. It is possible I will blunder."

"I have no concern in that regard," Ael said. Nonetheless, she was holding herself very still, determined not to tremble.

It is absurd. We have done this before. There was no harm done.

And I trust him.

He circled around behind the chair where she sat. This was the worst part, and Ael fought for calm. Very precisely his fingers positioned themselves over her nerve junctions, then touched her face. Ael took one long, shuddering breath and closed her eyes as, very slowly, another view of the world began overlaying itself on her own.

My mind to your mind. My thoughts . . . to your thoughts.

It had seemed impossible before, terrible, like insanity encroaching—another's voice in her own mind, another presence that spoke with her own voice, somehow thinking thoughts that were not hers. But they were slowly becoming hers. Slowly the sense of difference between herself and the other was dwindling. The back of her mind shrieked in protest at the loss of difference, but Ael was in no mood for it, and the terror receded.

. . . easier this time . . .

Yes, the answer came. *Our minds are drawing together.* She could feel the congruencies establishing themselves, similarities interlocking, differences respected and incorporated into the nearly established wholeness. *Closer still*—the whole compacting, slipping into phase—

Our minds are one. As if she needed telling now, with the flare of union, the astonished fire of synapses momentarily blinding her, a storm of thought and memory, the two streams of thought rushing together like two rivers in spate, eddies whirling and pouring into one another, a great rush of starfire and darkness, knowledge and uncertainty—

She saw now why her people had lost this art so long ago. Had the people of the Crossing, so enamored of pride, individuality, difference, their own chosen insularity from the rest of the species they left behind, come to reject this forced sharing-of-being as too high a price? Too undermining to the cherished sense of lonely individuality? For here, despite the vast gulf that separated her life from this other one, her upbringing and tendencies and her whole cast of mind, what was plain here was how alike, how very *alike* she and this other were, a great wash of similarities and resonances had risen to drown the differences. And the question arose before her: *Why in the Elements' names did we give this up?* Why did we walk away?

First see where you are. What must be done will become plain.

She stood in a darkness that shivered around its edges with red fire, and occupying the heart of the darkness was her other self's mind as it might appear in its solitary state, a cool but frighteningly complex weave of intellection, logic, and peace all interleaved with and woven into an equally complex, barbed, interconnected tangle of emotion, passion, and old buried violence. The logic was not an overlay, but a network, a matrix in which the older, dangerous substrates were embedded, held and managed, broken up and made relatively safe—though preserved for when they might be needed. This dangerous landscape leveled itself out before her as she gazed, while the force that held it all inside, the mind and will that bound it all up, watched to see what she would do.

She stepped out into it, over it, knowing that in so doing she would lay herself progressively more bare. The raging heat and aridity at the heart of that other worldview smote her with every step, tyrannous, partly a longing recollection of Vulcan's terrible heat, partly a paradigm for revelation, disclosure, layers of meaning burning and peeling away, revealing what lay beneath—

She gasped, but nonetheless moved forward over that dark and savage landscape, gazing down into its fires, and not so much seeing what lay within, but being seen by the source of the fires looking up and out at her. It perceived the image of Rihannsu space wrapped around her like a cloak, a great sweep of thousands of cubic light-years held all in mind despite its size, for after many years' service she knew it intimately. All that immense darkness was strung through with the implication of forces moving, men and minds and ships, though the knowledge was fragmentary, and all that space seemed to burn now with the sense of frustration at what was missing, what needed yet to be known. More was coming—when would it come?—it was not enough—

The anger will keep you from seeing clearly what must be done. You must let it go—

She pushed herself through the stifling heat and the darkness, feeling the layers of her own anger and terror burning away. It came hard, but for her people, for her own people on *Bloodwing* and for the innocents on ch'Rihan and ch'Havran and the colony worlds, she must have this, would have this, no matter how she suffered—

As if from out of the fires beneath her the glimpse erupted into her consciousness: the furious faces, shouting into hers, and at the edges of her mind, something tearing, pressing in, ripping at her as if with hooks—

She staggered on, unable to believe the intensity of the pain. It came and went in great bouts and waves, every one leaving the mind tenderer than the one before, and with an awful feeling of being raped, intruded into, that most intimate and secret place torn at and gored: ultimate violation—

Do not allow the circumstances to distract you. The mind-sifter is simply a mechanism that performs mind-meld without permission. It can be defeated in two ways. The first: by disengaging the pain, by denying it permission. The second requires a higher level of accomplishment. The first is accomplished by completely mastering the emotion: distaste, anger, but mostly fear—

She shuddered all over. *There. You see how the fear of what the pain will do is as bad as the pain itself, if allowed to persist. But both can be mastered—*

—there again, the leering faces, roaring with amusement, the questions, like hot iron, like cruelly spiked and unbearably heavy weights, pressing in intolerably from every side. She cried out in anguish. It seemed worse to feel it through him, with the experience reflecting back and forth inside their joined mind, doubled, quadrupled, than it would have felt had it simply been happening to her. She fought back against what was happening, tried to hold the pain at a distance—

You are reacting incorrectly. His instructor, or him? There was no telling: that meld was this meld . . . *This is not about resistance. The pain is part of what is really happening. To deny the truth is illogical. To accept it is the beginning of mastery. The pain must be accepted, and mastered, second by second, each second anew.*

She struggled along through the ever-increasing

burning, and suffered with him as he tried to achieve mastery in this most terrible situation, tried, failed. But tried again. And failed again, and tried again. And this time achieved it, finding his composure and adapting the techniques his instructor had shown him so long ago, not trying to stop the pain but accepting it wholly, including it, letting it pass through him, like a phaserblast through air; it vanishes, and the air closes around its path and is the air again, unbroken, untroubled. A flood of near disbelief, following the first second that the technique worked. But it *had* worked, though the next second the pain reasserted itself in all its fury. Again the air opens, includes it, lets it go by; and there is no pain. Again the pain; the air lets it pass; there is no pain . . .

There is no pain.

She fastened on that phrase, hope flaring in her, for now she felt his experience as he did, knew for sure that he had done it, had survived, and with his mind and his secrets intact. *But there is more to it than that,* the other self said. *The words do not describe what you are making happen, but what has* already *happened. Resistance is not how the pain is overcome. Resistance implies that there* exists *something else which must second by second be resisted. This phenomenology will defeat you, leaving you at the mercy of the pain. But to master the pain, it must be included, accepted. Then it vanishes, then there truly is no pain—*

Understood.

Is it indeed? Let us see.

Sickbay—

Diane Duane

Her mind went up in a flare of anguish and fear. She would not look at that. *I have paid that price. I pay it again every day. I will not pay in that coinage now!*

Then prevent this.

The terrible pain came and tore at her part of the joined mind, efficiently, fiercely—though not mercilessly. It was not a machine, though it was acting like one, for her sake. And she knew, too, as she strove to deal with the pain, that whatever she might say, *he* was paying in such a coinage. To some extent, every mind-meld recalled every other. She heard echoes: *if only I could forget . . . to the death, or life for both of us! . . . cry for the children, weep for the murdered ones! . . .* and many another. And they were all cries of pain. *Ah, it is ill named mind-meld,* Ael thought in anguish. *Heart-meld would be closer—*

The children. That echo, wordless, seemed somehow more immediate than the others. There had been some resonance between the mother Horta and her children, even while they were still in the egg, that her other self had sensed without clearly understanding. Were Hortas at all telepathic? Possibly no more so than humans or Rihannsu, but suddenly Ael perceived the lake of lava burning against the darkness of the Horta homeworld's great depths, and saw the skin of cooling stone across the top of it hardening, going cold and dark, and then breaking and shattering with the flow of the lava beneath it, cracks widening, the liquid fire oozing up, cooling and darkening again. That was the path she had to traverse, the paradigm through which she had to move. The lava was the pain, which always would break through. But the pain itself could be subverted again and again, the energy diverted from it, so that it would go cold; and over that surface one could safely walk—

She swallowed, feeling the rising tide of agony. *Or instead, one might accept it wholly,* she thought. *How often have I pushed it aside, for the sake of duty . . . or fear?*

No more.

She walked out to where the lava crust broke, and the terrible scorching heat of it blasted up at her from the molten stone, blazing, so that her skin went tight with it and her eyes stung, watering terribly.

No more . . .

And she leaped.

Sickbay.

The rage, the pain, the agony, more intense than she had ever felt before, than she had ever *allowed* herself to feel before, now swallowed her whole in a blaze of white-hot fire that molded itself to her like a terrible new flesh, devouring the flesh beneath it. *My son . . .*

Not my son! He could not have betrayed—

—weep for the children!—

The lava finished burning her flesh away, charred her bones, eating inward . . .

What did I do wrong? How has he done this to them, to me?!

—cry for the murdered ones!—

Dead at my hand. Not his own. Mine. I am responsible.

—eyes burning, skull alight, the brain flashing into final fire—

Oh my Element, would that I had died instead of him!

There was nothing left of her. It was over.

Sorrow . . . for the end of things.

Finished . . .

. . . when she noticed that the pain was gone, and she was swimming in blazing light that blinded her, but hurt her not at all.

And then she was alone.

She blinked. Behind her, she heard someone move—*felt* him move, without having to look. It was Spock, coming around to face her, leaning against the desk.

"It is done," he said. He straightened, trying to look casual about it, but she knew perfectly well what effort the last few minutes had cost him. They had felt like years.

For her own part Ael wiped her face and sat still for several moments, trying to find her composure again. "You are a harsh teacher, Mr. Spock," Ael said.

He shook his head. "On the contrary, Commander. I merely showed you the path. You walked it . . . and further than the need of the moment required."

"I would not be sure of that," Ael said.

"I would."

She could find no answer. "The paradigm you

chose was an unusual one," Spock said, "but since it
was of your choosing, I believe it will serve you
well. Recall it to yourself daily, by way of reinforc-
ing it. Meanwhile, if circumstances allow, a second
session within several days might be wise, in order
to check that the routine has been correctly installed
and implemented."

She was half tempted to laugh, hearing him speak
as dryly of her mind as of a computer into which he
had been loading new software. But the metaphor
was probably apt. "As you say, that will be as circumstances permit. But for the moment . . ."

Ael got up slowly, a little stiff from sitting a long
time tensed in that chair. She cast around in her
mind to see how things felt. Her sense of herself was
normal again, save for that thin persistent thread of
connectedness between them, carrying at the moment no overheard content, no remotely sensed im-
agery—just the knowledge that it was *there*. Last
time it had faded quickly; this time she was not quite
sure how long it might remain.

Words to describe any of the many things she
presently felt eluded her utterly. All Ael could do
was bow to him and hold the bow—as she had for
Jim, but for different reasons—three full breaths'
worth. She might have held it longer, but she felt his
fingers brush her arm, and she straightened.

He had neither moved nor reached out to her. As
Ael looked up at him again, she caught an echo, so
indistinct she thought she had not been meant to hear
it, and very distant: *touching . . . never touched . . .*

"Use it well, Commander," Spock said. "Or rather: so live and prosper that you need never use it at all."

Ael went out and found Mr. Naraht waiting for her. She smiled at him with more than the usual affection, though she did not tell him why. When the *Enterprise*'s transporter room glowed out of existence to be replaced by *Bloodwing*'s, suddenly the weariness hit her full force, and she stumbled down off the pads like one caught between dream and waking. The doors opened, and Aidoann was there. She opened her mouth to say something, but she checked herself and came forward hurriedly to take Ael by the arms and steady her. *"Khre'Riov,"* Aidoann said, and then more softly, "Ael, in Fire's name, what's come to you? You look like you've seen a ghost."

Ael shook her head and tried to laugh, but a weak, shaky laugh it was that came out. "So I have," she said. "I may yet see many more such, but they and I will hereafter learn to be more at peace with one another, perhaps." She straightened up, and this time her voice found something of the accustomed steadiness again. "However that may be, the living will be enough trouble for us in the next while, cousin—so let's go finish setting our ship in order. In just a few hours, the enemy will be at the gate . . ."

Chapter Seven

RV TRIANGULI was an A3 giant, something of a loner as stars went. It had no planets—just an asteroid belt about 14 AU out—and its only other claim to fame was its classification as a star of the delta Scuti type, a variable with a difference. *Enterprise* came coasting in past its radiopause, the primary's actinic blue-white fire blazing with ever-increasing brilliance on her hull, and on those of *Sempach* and *Nimrod* to either side. The increase in the brilliance was not entirely because they were coming closer to it: as they approached, the star could be seen to be gently swelling. Somewhere out there, at a comfortable distance from the star, the Romulans were waiting with the other Federation starships, and Jim found himself hoping the sight of RV made them twitch. It certainly had that effect on *him*.

Jim was coming back up from engineering on the

way to the bridge when he met Spock at the turbo-lift. "Anything from *Hemalat* or *Lake Champlain?*" he asked as they got into the lift.

"They are in position, and the Romulan vessels are all present and accounted for," Spock said. "Bridge. Apparently the initial meeting went without incident; translator upgrades were exchanged."

"Good. See to it that Uhura gets what she needs."

"Additionally," Spock said, "*Ortisei* and *Blood-wing* have left for the neighborhood of 38 Tri . . . though officially, of course, we do not know that is where they have gone."

Jim nodded. "Any new insights into your, ah, 'meeting' with her?"

Spock looked thoughtful. "Not as such. But regarding your interest in the ship movements and planetary mobilizations I perceived in her memory—there is no possibility of error as regards their genuineness, Captain."

"Unless she's being deluded about them too."

"I rate that probability as very low."

"How low? Zero?"

Spock gave Jim one of those "you know better than that" looks. "Sorry, Mr. Spock," Jim said, "but the stakes are a lot higher than usual this time out. I need to know how strong a hand I'm betting on."

"I would say the odds on the commander being correct in her particulars are significantly better than those for drawing to an inside straight," Spock said, "as I observed you doing at the open game in the recreation room nine days ago. With predictable results."

"Ouch," Jim said. There seemed no point in mentioning that it had seemed like a good idea at the time. "Noted and logged."

The lift doors opened. "Captain," Uhura said, *"Speedwell* has arrived. The 'neutral ground' vessel is coming in with her."

"Oh, the Lalairu ship," Jim said. The Romulans had been somewhat uneasy about meeting with the Federation delegation on a Starfleet vessel or Federation world, and—though he would not have said so out loud—Jim suspected the Federation complement had similar concerns about walking into a Romulan ship. Therefore both sides had agreed that the actual meetings would take place aboard a vessel of the Lalairu, an independent "family" of species who favored the traveling lifestyle—a species well known for not favoring any one large interstellar bloc over another, and for going their own way, neutral but most seriously armed, preferring to take care of themselves in the empty spaces rather than depend on the protection of federations or empires. The Lalairu had been willing to assist the two parties and had had a ship out this way. Jim was particularly fascinated by this aspect of the meetings; he had never seen a Lalairu ship, though like most other people he had heard about them.

Now *Enterprise* coasted in close to that brilliant sun, ten million miles out or so, and away past it again, as RV Trianguli continued to swell, like some huge creature taking in a breath, and taking it in, and taking it in . . . Jim looked at it on the bridge viewscreen with faint unease as he sat down. "That's not a star that could be successfully seeded, is it, Spock?"

Spock, standing behind the center seat for the moment, raised his eyebrows. "It would be a problematic endeavor, Captain," he said. "While it is in the 'possible' range as far as stellar class is concerned, the mere fact of its variability would complicate matters considerably. Add to the equation the nature of its variability—three different 'variation' cycles running at once, so that its luminosity increases and decreases by a full magnitude every thirty-three hours, by two-tenths of a magnitude every five hours, and by six-tenths of a magnitude every fourteen hours—" He shook his head. "This star's upper atmosphere is already unstable enough. I would be forced to conclude that anyone willing to tamper with it could be judged suicidal."

"We'll hope everybody else sees it your way, Mr. Spock," Jim said softly. "All the same . . ." He trailed off. There were plenty of other Starfleet vessels here, but he would be keeping an eye on that star regardless.

The star fell away behind them, and Mr. Sulu changed the view for one forward. Way out in the system one could barely make out a faint dusting of light, a long thin diffuse band stretched across the darkness: the star's asteroid belt, a densely populated region indeed to judge by the fact that it could be seen at all at this distance, with so little magnification. "Was that a planet once, do you think?"

"There has been no research done that I am aware

of," Spock said, heading over to his scanner and bending to peer down into it, "but the conjecture would not be out of the bounds of possibility. Though it is rare for Delta Scuti stars to produce planets at all. The question of greatest interest would be, if it *had* been a planet, what caused the fragmentation?" He worked with the scanner for a moment, then said, "Total mass of material in present orbit would suggest a planet originally about twice the size of Earth, or two-thirds that of Vulcan. Composition mostly the lighter elements. To judge by a sampling of the residue, the core was small and low in metals. More like Vulcan than Earth." Spock straightened up again, looking at the viewscreen, where that dust of light was beginning to resolve itself into a chain of faint, faint sparks. "Whatever happened to it would have been a major event. I would hope there might be time to investigate further."

Another gleam of light showed up off to one side of the forward view: the characteristically brief but splendid light trail of a starship dropping out of warp and "braking" hard, the superluminal particles she had carried with her inside her warp field now hitting the inflexible barrier of c and destroying themselves in a brief and furious deceleration rainbow as the field collapsed. As she approached, Jim counted four nacelles: another *Constellation*-class ship. It was *Speedwell,* a shade late, as Danilov had predicted, but in good enough time.

"*Speedwell* is hailing us, Captain," Uhura said.

"Put them on."

The viewscreen shimmered into a view of the new arrival's bridge. In the center seat sat a handsome woman of medium height and build, with short, fluffy silver hair, a round, cheerful face, and the devil in her blue eyes. Jim stood up, as much out of respect as for the fact that the newcomer was a woman, and said, "Captain Helgasdottir."

"Captain Kirk," Birga Helgasdottir said, inclining her head to him a little. "A pleasure to meet you at last. Even if we do have to do it here at the back end of nowhere."

"If nothing else," Jim said, "the background won't be boring."

"No, I'd have to agree with you there. I look forward to having the leisure to get to know you better. Meanwhile, Captain, I have someone here who wanted to greet you before we met the rest of the group and got down to business." She glanced to one side.

A big, burly man in the restrained silver-gray of the Federation's "commissioned" diplomatic corps stepped into view. Jim was surprised. "Ambassador Fox!" he said. "Don't tell me you're finally *finished* at Eminiar VII—"

The man actually laughed, a sound Jim wouldn't have thought he had in him when they first met. Robert Fox looked much as he had when he had first become involved in the negotiations between Eminiar and Vendikar, though perhaps a little more silvery at the temples and a little wearier. As far as Jim knew, he had been stuck for at least the last few years in a bout of shuttlecraft diplomacy between the two worlds that had looked like it would become a permanent thing. "Finished?" he said. "Captain, I'm pretty good at my job, but not *that* good. I've been training my replacement for a while now. Apparently the Federation thought this would be a good time to see if he's learned anything, and to send me off for a change of pace."

"You'll get that," Jim said, "in spades. How are things going between Eminiar and Vendikar?"

"Oh, they've got a ways to go yet before people from either side feel comfortable going for vacations on each other's planets," Fox said, sounding rueful. "But it's no surprise. All those centuries of war have left them with a lot of pain. The hostilities proper may be over, but the hostility isn't. They have a lot to unlearn."

"But they're on their way."

"They are," Fox said. "When they found out where I was going, though, they specifically asked me to greet you for them."

Jim put his eyebrows up at that. "How would they have known *I'd* be here?"

Fox smiled slightly. "Where the Romulans are involved," he said, "I don't think anyone would expect this particular meeting to happen without you and *Enterprise* at least somewhere in the background—if not rather more centrally placed. Even though the news that's gotten out to the public services has been somewhat, shall we say, controlled, there's a lot of speculation out there at the moment. And some

Diane Duane

people are guessing right about what's happening."

Jim nodded. "Well, Ambassador," he said, "I hope we have some time to sit down and talk between actual proceedings."

"I suspect we will. Captain?" Fox turned to Helgasdottir.

She turned her attention back to the viewscreen from the yeoman who had just presented her with a padd of orders to sign. "Well, Captain, we'll see you in a few hours at the informal session. We need to clear in the vessel we've been escorting."

"Certainly, Captain. Until later."

The screen flicked back to the view of the stars again, and the asteroid belt now even closer, as Sulu dumped *Enterprise*'s speed right down to impulse. *Speedwell* matched her, alongside, and Jim sat back down.

Spock came down to stand behind the center seat. "I must confess it is something of a surprise to see *Speedwell* here at all," he said. "Her late engagements at 302 Ceti and the Anduath uprising were a considerable distance away."

"You have a talent for understatement, Mr. Spock," Jim said. "But somehow it's not a surprise to me." *The eagles are gathering,* Jim thought. *Danilov and Helgasdottir here together: they could have had a war all by themselves. And probably would, if allowed.*

Jim looked at the screen, where the asteroids were now a chain of tiny stars. One of the documents Ael had left for him to look at had been a list of the

72

major names likely to be appearing for the Romulans in the discussions about to start, and with few exceptions the only balance for which they seemed to have been chosen was one which weighed down hard on one side against the Federation in every way that mattered. Poor Fox was going to have his work cut out for him.

The bridge doors opened and McCoy came in, stepping down to stand off to one side of the center seat. "Is everybody here who's supposed to be here?" he said.

"So *Sempach* says, Doctor," Spock said, "though it will be a few seconds yet before we have visual without magnification." He stepped back to his scanner and looked down into it. "There are six Romulan vessels in system, IDs coming in now—" He broke off.

Jim turned around. "Something quite massive dropping out of warp," Spock said. "Very close—"

The viewscreen blazed with rainbow light as a shining ovoid shape came plunging in along the vector *Speedwell* had used, bremsstrahlung fire sleeting and sheeting away from it, dying back to leave only the fierce sheen of RV's light on what was now revealed as a great, sleek, egg-shaped hull. Behind Jim, McCoy's hands tightened on the back of the center seat.

"What in Beelzebub's name is *that?*" McCoy said.

The huge thing decelerated hard and fast, and seemingly without effort, slipping up to ride behind and above *Speedwell* and matching her speed and

Enterprise's perfectly. It was like being paced by a small moon. "That," Jim said, "is the neutral vessel. The Lalairu ship."

It filled the entire viewscreen in aft view; a massive and perfectly symmetrical "egg" of plasteel, which reflected the glare of RV Tri in some places and let it through, somewhat diminished, in others. "Look at the size of that thing!" McCoy said in a hushed voice. "I bet it gets to be neutral anywhere it wants. How many crew are *in* there?"

"I don't know how many of them are crew as such," Uhura said, "but there are about nine thousand entities aboard, of all kinds of species. Then again the Lalairu aren't a single species, anyway, but a family . . . and by their standards, that's probably not so much a ship as a city. It IDs itself as *Mascrar.*"

"I hope they do not expect us to take care of them if trouble breaks out," Chekov muttered.

"On the contrary, Mr. Chekov," Spock said, "the Lalairu are most likely more heavily armed than any of us, and 'if trouble breaks out' they will take whatever measures are necessary to see that it does not affect them."

Mascrar continued to follow behind them, demure but impossible to ignore, and the *Enterprise* slipped in closer to where the other ships were awaiting her. Well this side of the asteroid belt, there were *Lake Champlain* and *Hemalat* hanging in the darkness, with *Sempach* and *Nimrod* decelerating to take a stand with them. And there, at a little distance, were the Romulan ships.

Jim got up from the center seat again and folded his arms, looking at them. "One quarter impulse, Mr. Sulu," he said. "Bring us in to park with the others."

"Aye, sir."

"Is it just me," McCoy said from behind him, "or do those ships look bigger than the ones we've seen before?"

"Some of them," Jim said, "yes." It looked to Jim as if someone in the Romulan space services had decided it was time to update their "signature" design somewhat. In the newer ships—*replacements,* Jim thought rather unrepentantly, *for ones we blew up at Levaeri V*—someone had taken the original flattish bird-of-prey design and decided to go for curves instead of angles. The curves drooped downward, as did the bows of the ships, giving them a look that still made you think of some big predatory bird, but one with a more lowering, dangerous quality to it. Jim smiled a little grimly. Whoever had been at work on these ships knew one of the rules of starship design: if you were designing warships as such, you should try to make them look to your enemy like something he or she would prefer not to tangle with. Worse, for someone who knew the old bird-of-prey designs, these suggested that the designers were hinting at some kind of secret—one that was not going to be in *your* best interests. And these were not merely takeoffs on Klingon ship design, either; this particular look bore a different kind of threat.

"Interesting," Spock said. "This transitional de-

75

sign would seem to suggest that they too are experimenting with warp field augmentation . . ."

"Better than our newer ships, you think?" Jim said.

"It is difficult to tell at first glance," Spock said. "Certainly we are meant to think so." He was already stepping back to his scanner to get some readings. "But the hull design is suggestive . . . And here are the ship IDs for you, Captain. *Gorget* is that largest one, and its companion of the same class is *Thraiset.* The others are *Saheh'lill, Greave, Pillion,* and *Hheirant.*"

They were mostly new names to Jim. But a lot of the older Romulan ships with which he was familiar, ships with which he and *Enterprise* had skirmished in the past, were gone following the events of the last few months—the notable exception being *Bloodwing.*

Jim went back to the center seat and glanced at McCoy in passing. "Is this pre-meeting formal dress?" the doctor asked, rubbing his neck meditatively.

"Afraid so, Bones," Jim said as he sat down again. "It's the tight collars for both of us."

"As long as it's nothing tighter," Bones said, looking at the Romulan ships with slight unease. "Though last time we met, they were more likely to shoot me than hang me, as I remember."

"The Lalairu take their neutrality very seriously, Doctor," Jim said. "If the Romulans tried to kill you, they'd almost immediately have cause to be extremely sorry."

"Not half as sorry as *I* would be," McCoy muttered.

Uhura looked up at that. "The city manager of *Mascrar,* the Laihe as it calls itself, would like to meet briefly with the Federation negotiating team and the captains of the on-site ships about an hour before the first informal meeting with the Romulans, Captain. Just to restate the conditions under which the negotiations are taking place and to clear up any last-minute difficulties."

"That's fine, Lieutenant," said Jim. "Tell it we'll be there." He got up and headed for the lift. "I may as well go get changed."

The Lalairu vessel turned out to be as spectacular inside as outside. Because of all the species that made up the Lalairu extended family, their architecture was a farrago of the styles and mannerisms of many worlds, sometimes bizarrely blended, sometimes welded into a surprisingly effective unity, considering the unlikeness, or unlikeliness, of the component parts when taken separately. The city inside the egg-shaped structure was arranged around a core "spindle" that ran from one end to the other of the ovoid, and buildings—spires and domes and arches of every shape and kind—were arranged right around that cylinder, so that the huge airy inside of the egg looked as if someone had stuffed a bottle-brush into it. Everything glittered with light, not just from RV Trianguli but from the interior lights inside the outer shell that came on to maintain minimum light levels for the parts of the city that were rotating into darkness.

The building where the captains and the Federation team were meeting was at the far end of one spindle, near the top of a spire that jutted from the end of it. As they materialized inside it, McCoy was muttering, "Don't know how this thing stays where it *is*, Spock. You'd think it would have to be fastened somewhere."

"Doubtless it is secured, Doctor," Spock said, "but by inertial pressors and other such non-visible mechanisms. There are, after all, Hamalki among the Lalairu, not to mention Sulamids and members of other species that have great reputations as builders and engineers." Jim glanced around him at the space in which they now stood—a circular room about fifty meters in diameter, completely surrounded by floor-to-ceiling windows, and containing what seemed to be a small forest of trees reaching to within several meters of the ceiling, some twenty meters up. The ceiling proper glowed with warm, golden artificial light suggestive of a K- or G-type star. In the middle of the "forest" was a large, irregular circle of various kinds of comfortable seating, in muted colors. At the center of the circle stood the Laihe.

Jim made his way over to it with the other captains and their executive crew. The Laihe was a humanoid, though an unusual one—most likely a member of a species native to a low-gravity world, to judge by its extreme slenderness and its height, nearly three meters. Its skin was ebony black, its eyes and long shaggy mane of hair a gold that almost perfectly matched the color of the ceiling light, and it was clothed in a coverall of some material that managed to look more like topaz-colored glass than anything else, transparent in some places and translucent in others, but not the usual ones. As the Federation group approached, it bowed to them, a graceful, curving gesture that took its head right down to the ground and up again to look at them with those golden eyes.

"Gentlebeings, you are welcome to the city *Mascrar*," the Laihe said. "I am the city manager."

"May we ask how we should properly address you?" said Commodore Danilov.

"We give up personal names during our term of office. Laihe is the only name I have right now—besides the ones people call me in the course of business." The Laihe produced an expression which by hominid standards would pass for a smile, but was so edged with irony that Jim suspected that in emergencies it could be used to shave with. "In any case, I thank you for agreeing to meet with me before the main event begins. Will you all sit?"

Everyone sorted themselves out into the kind of seating that best fitted their physiology. "I just wanted to make sure that we had everyone's understanding of the physical arrangements for the discussions," the Laihe said, seating itself also. "For the time being we would ask your group of ships to stay on the opposite side of our city from the one where the Romulans are orbiting. There have occasionally been breakdowns in communication in such circumstances, and when discussions of such delicacy are in train, for the sake of our own reputation as facilitators, we prefer that the aggressor be easily determined from the start—by putting ourselves in the line of fire, and thereby ensuring we are best able to judge from which direction fire initially came." It smiled that barbed smile again. "Naturally we will respond robustly to any such occurrence. I mention it merely in passing, since you obviously would not be the cause of such a situation."

"Of course not," Commodore Danilov said. Jim had to smile slightly, for he had a strong feeling that the Laihe had used exactly the same wording with the Romulans. "And we appreciate your willingness to assist both sides in this matter."

"You are most welcome," the Laihe said. "The formal discussions are scheduled to begin ten standard hours from now, in another part of this building, which is our 'city hall.' Coordinates will be provided for you, and we will pass a broadcast of the proceedings to each ship for dissemination to involved personnel. If the various captains will coordinate with our communications center and sort out the details, I would take it very kindly. Meanwhile, is there anything with which the city can assist you? Do you have everything you need to carry out your business here?"

There were murmurs of thanks and polite refusal from most of the captains. Jim glanced around and said, "Laihe, I would appreciate an exchange of ship's libraries, if possible."

"My pleasure," the Laihe said. "There is no higher aspiration than the preservation and distribution of knowledge." It smiled again, a less barbed look this time. "But then I am a Telkandai, and I *would* say that. I will gladly coordinate with your science officer in this matter."

"Thank you, Laihe."

"Is there anything else, gentlemen and ladies? No?" The Laihe rose again. "Then let us repair to the informal meeting. Your opposite numbers will be arriving there now. The transporter pads are over this way."

It led them through several small spinneys of trees into a niche where a good-sized multiple transport pad was sited, and led the first group of Starfleet officers onto it. Jim hung back a little, letting them go with the Laihe, and as they shimmered away, Bones leaned a little closer to him and muttered, "Was that a *warning*, you think?"

"A tactful one, anyway," Jim said. His mind was on something he had been reading the night before, and the warning struck him as unusually apropos. "They're not a trigger-happy people, at any rate. I wouldn't be overly worried, Bones. They've never been involved in the beginning of a war."

"First time for everything," McCoy muttered as they stepped up onto the pads themselves.

The shimmer took them out of the "forest" room and into a place where the lighting was dimmer, more subtle. Jim stepped down off the pads . . . and took a long breath.

The word *room* would have been a poor description for where they were now. The place stood at the top of the spire—the very top. It was surrounded by inward-leaning walls of something transparent—

clearsteel, glass, or plex—from the floor to the
spearing ceiling: the view beyond was of the stars
and nothing else. The outer walls of the city-ship at
this end had, for the moment at least, lost their re-
flective quality, and the stars showed through
clearly. They circled around the cynosure of the
peak-spire as if around a polestar. No matter how
angry or nervous any being had been on entering
that room, it had to stop and gaze up, and if it had so
much as a breath of wonder in it, it would stop and
let that breath out, for the view was dazzling.

Jim let his own breath out, very impressed indeed.
Then he looked across the huge room and saw the
Romulans there, waiting.

They were gathered fairly close together, as if trying to present a united front. Some of them were
glaring at the Federation people; others looked non-
chalant. Some were sneaking repeat glances at that
amazing view. They were all splendidly dressed,
some in formal robes and cloaks along vaguely Vulcan lines, others in the dark uniforms of the Romulan armed forces or space forces—tunics and
breeches or skirts or kilts of various lengths, usually
topped with diagonal or vertical sashes of subtly
glittering colors. Jim knew enough about Rihannsu
uniform conventions after consulting with Ael to realize that some of the people here were very senior
indeed, in either the military or civilian mode. They
were apparently intent on not insulting anyone by
sending negotiators of inadequate rank.

"Buffet tables over there look pretty good,"

McCoy said. "Do we have to wait for introductions or something?"

"I am sure the Laihe would have mentioned such a necessity," Spock said. "I would guess you may by all means feel free to go indulge your appetites."

Bones snorted. "Thanks a lot." He paused, then smiled slightly. "Think I'll mosey on over there and annoy a couple of people."

"Oh?" Jim said. "Doctor, don't get us off to a bad start here. Who did you have in mind?"

"See that tall lady in the dark robe with the green sash?" Jim nodded. The woman was easily one of the tallest members of the group of about twenty. She was striking, with high cheekbones and long, very dark red hair, and looked like a candidate for the recently vacated position of Wicked Witch of the West.

"The sash," McCoy said, "is for a blood feud presently ongoing. With *you,* Jim. That's the wife of *Battlequeen*'s late commander. A praetor, and hence pretty much at the head of the line of people who wanted to see what color my liver was, a month or so ago. Hloal t'Illialhlae, her name is."

Jim nodded. He remembered her from McCoy's report, and now privately thought that he had not understated the woman's potential dangerousness. It was always unwise to assume too much about facial expressions across hominid species, but humans and Rihannsu were alike enough in some regards that Jim was pretty sure t'Illialhlae did not have his best interests, or *Enterprise*'s, at heart. "If she hands me a drink," he said softly, "I'll let you scan it first."

"I fear the Lalairu would not appreciate that, Captain," Spock said. "They have guaranteed our safety while we are under their roof."

"I'll grant you, it's some roof," McCoy said, glancing up. "But all the same, I won't let her serve the punch while *I'm* nearby. Speaking of which . . ."

He headed off across the room. Jim, for his own part, glanced around among the final group of Federation people arriving, and as Ambassador Fox headed past Jim toward the Romulan delegation, Jim suddenly caught sight in the ambassador's group of a face he had been expecting to see, though he hadn't been sure of exactly when. A small man with sandy hair and a wrinkled, genial face, wearing a beige and brown singlesuit that looked as if it had been applied to him with a shovel, and carrying the unmistakable telltale: a big book under one arm. The sharp eyes in that face caught Jim's and lit up.

"Sam!"

Samuel T. Cogley, Esquire, headed across the acreage of floor toward Jim, reached out, and shook him vigorously by the hand. "Been too damn long," he said. "Too long by half. Hello there, Mr. Spock! Nice to see you. How are you, Jim?"

"Concerned by the circumstances and the surroundings," Jim said as they walked off a little way, and he nodded for Spock to come with them, "but otherwise, fine. How've you been?"

"Oh, a little busy, working on this case," said Cogley. "After all, asylum law was hardly a specialty for me. But it's like anything else—you start getting interested, and then it's too late . . ."

Jim chuckled. When it had become obvious how things were going, he had strongly suggested to Ael that she was going to need some form of help on the Federation side that did not have phasers attached to it. "Certainly," she had said, "if you know someone who handles lost causes . . ." Jim had grinned and immediately sent off a message to the best handler of lost causes he knew.

Afterwards he'd gotten a sneaking feeling that Starfleet might have preferred some other defender at these proceedings, but there was nothing they could do about it when Sam Cogley volunteered his services. Merely knowing and having successfully defended James T. Kirk was not enough to disqualify a counselor who was known for many other successful if positively quirky defenses here and there in Federation space. In fact, there were certainly people in Fleet who would have taken Cogley's involvement as a sign that the best that had been done—was being done—for Ael, and they were perfectly willing to let him go ahead, since the chances were better than even that the best might not be good enough.

"Have you had a chance to look over the preliminary paperwork?" Jim said.

Sam put his eyebrows up. "I've done better than that," he said. "I did opening submissions earlier today."

"What?"

Sam smiled slightly and steered Jim and Spock toward one of the great windows. "There's already been an initial session," Cogley said, very quietly. "It's usually the case in proceedings like this. The diplomats involved, the real ones or their representatives rather than the negotiators of title, try to get together and do a little sorting out before the official sessions start. Fox sent an assistant in early with instructions; the Romulans did the same. Establishing ground rules, feeling out the sentiments of the other party . . . the usual."

"Without telling *us?*" Jim muttered.

"It's how business gets done," Sam said.

Jim let out a long breath. "Well, we're just here as enforcement, really," he said. "I suppose it shouldn't surprise me that we hear about things a little late."

"That's true. But I'll keep you posted as best I can," Sam said. "Though we don't want to spend too much time together in public, so let's keep this brief. Anyway, things are already going moderately well. I was able to throw a few procedural *sabots* into the machinery earlier. Though apparently that suits Fox's intentions at the moment."

"Diplomacy," Spock said, "is after all the art of prolonging a conflict."

"Prolonging it at the jaw-flapping stage, instead of the photon torpedo and phaser stage," Sam said, "yes, indeed. If today's been anything to go by, we're doing well in that regard. We spent the better part of an hour just attempting to settle whether Commander-General t'Rllaillieu was extraditable."

Jim was slightly surprised. "I would have thought she was."

"Oh, that wouldn't be at all certain." Sam smiled with pure enjoyment. "See, the concept of extradition requires *ab initio* that the two jurisdictions agree in recognizing the action in question as a crime. Not the action as a *class*, mind you: the Federation side rejected that out of hand."

"You mean you rejected it and they jumped on the bandwagon."

"When the band's playing the right tune," Cogley said, "sometimes it's hard to resist. But the Federation's reaction to what happened at Levaeri V, when the Romulans started complaining to them about the destruction of their ships and their space station and its personnel, was fairly straightforward. Their immediate counterquestion was: 'Well, what were you doing with all that Vulcan brain tissue? Oh, and now that we think of it, exactly what were you doing with the starship *Intrepid?*' " Sam grinned. "From the Starfleet point of view, there wasn't any crime committed. *Enterprise* and *Inaieu* and the other ships went in to recover our hijacked personnel and materials. Then the Romulans said, 'But this woman has stolen one of our starships. We want it back.' 'Ah,' Starfleet says, through Fox and his cronies, 'but she's applied for political asylum here, stating that what she did was an act of resistance against a corrupt government, and that she used no more than reasonable force to allow her and her crew to escape. And naturally all her crew have filed for asylum as well, and are backing her up in their testimony.' "

Jim said nothing for the moment. The reality was

Diane Duane

a little more hazy, for Ael had applied for nothing, as he understood it. Starfleet's agreement with her that she could take refuge in Federation space had been an informal one. *They wanted to pump her for information about the Imperium,* Jim thought, *and didn't find her terribly forthcoming at that point, so they never went any further in formally confirming the privilege.* It was a matter that had made Ael, as Jim understood it, somewhat uncomfortable—not that she would ever reveal that discomfort to Starfleet. But now apparently someone had produced documentation to suggest that a request for asylum had been formally made and accepted. Or else someone had implied that such documentation existed.

Very, very interesting . . .

"Look, Sam," Jim said, "stay in touch. We're not going anywhere, and I'll really be wanting to hear your slant on this thing as it unfolds."

Sam nodded, glancing sideways to see Commodore Danilov rather stiffly and quietly greeting Hloal t'Illialhae, who herself seemed to be concentrating on keeping her face an absolute mask as she spoke. She might as well not have bothered: the way she was holding the rest of her body suggested her loathing and fury all too clearly. "I can understand that," he said. "I'll do what I can for you, and for her. But one thing, Jim. If there are going to be any sudden moves, let me know."

Jim nodded. "Do my best."

Sam took himself away toward Fox's group. Jim

looked after him as he went, and said to Spock, "I didn't see what the book was."

Spock's expression was difficult to read. "It was *The Lives of the Martyrs.*"

Jim let out a breath. "Huh," he said. "Well, come on, Mr. Spock. Let's eat, drink, and be merry, for to-morrow—"

Spock favored him with a look suggesting that he found the quote profoundly inappropriate.

They headed for the buffet tables nonetheless. Jim was aware that it would probably be unwise for him to make a first move toward the Romulans. Like the other captains, he was aware that he was here on suf-ferance—for the rest of the negotiations he and the others would be aboard their ships, since their pres-ence at the proceedings would certainly have been seen as potentially provocative by one side or the other. For the moment, Jim busied himself briefly with making a small tidy sandwich with some grilled and "pulled" stayf—heaven only knew where the Lalairu were getting stayf; for all Jim knew, they were cloning it themselves—and watching what McCoy would have referred to as "the group dy-namic."

It was uncomfortable. At first the two groups did not have much to do with each other; each stayed mostly gathered to itself, looking at the others and making no overt move toward them. *Caution, or xenophobia, under the guise of nonintrusiveness,* Jim thought. *Or a desire to have a more structured environment in which to meet than this . . .* But the Lalairu were making no attempt whatever to bring the two sides together. Possibly they might have thought it a violation of their neutral role. Or perhaps they were simply wise enough to realize that sooner or later, curiosity would do for both sides what amity would have done in a less loaded situation.

Fox, for his own part, was talking to a small, slender man in Romulan ground-forces uniform whom Jim did not recognize. He committed the man's face to memory for the moment—dossiers with pictures and vids would doubtless be making the rounds shortly—and turned his attention elsewhere, to that tall, striking woman t'Illialhlae, again. It was truly astonishing how hostile she could look, how deadly. *If she bit me, I'd want shots right then,* he thought, trying to remember whether Ael had said anything about her. He couldn't remember offhand, but the thought of shots suddenly made him wonder what McCoy was up to. And come to think of it, where was Spock? He had drifted off while Jim was assembling his second sandwich.

Before he got started looking around, Jim moved over to one of the tables where drinks were laid out, picked up a decanter, and was pouring himself a small tot of Romulan ale when he felt a shadow fall over him. He looked up.

Blocking the starlight was one of the tallest Romulans he had ever seen, a big bear of a man in an older-style military uniform with a sort of floor-length dark green tabard over it. The man had short bristly hair and a craggy, fierce, broken-nosed face. He was looking at Jim with an expression that, while hostile, seemed to embody an amiable kind of hostility, like that of one who admired the handsome colors of a bug prior to stepping on it.

Jim straightened up and reacted to the look the only way he could, holding up the crystal decanter from which he had been pouring. "Ale, sir?"

Those dark, angry eyes widened a little, and then the man bowed to him a little and said, "I take that very kindly." He held out his glass.

"Say when."

The man looked at him oddly. "Why?"

"I'm sorry, sir. I mean, tell me how much of this you'd like."

The rough face split in a grin. "More than it would be wise for me to drink, at the moment. Half the glass, if you would."

Jim poured, privately considering that the day he drank that much of the blue stuff at one sitting would only be the day on which McCoy finally worked out the bugs in the removable-brain routine for humans. He briefly considered topping up his own glass and ditching it after he and this man parted company, then shrugged and put the decanter down.

Jim raised his glass. "Your health," he said.

The Romulan studied him. "That's something it surprises me that you would wish for."

"Common courtesy," Jim said, "would seem to suggest it. Other healths used by officers of previous services"—he smiled—"would seem to be inappropriate here."

"And what healths would those be?"

"Well, a typical one, in armed services where the officers did not usually advance much in position in peacetime, would be, 'To a sudden plague or a bloody war.'"

There was a pause, and then a great guffaw of laughter. It startled Jim, for he had never heard such a sound from a Romulan before. He had to laugh too, just at the sound of it; it was infectious.

"Maybe," the Romulan said, "maybe I see what the damned traitress sees in you."

"You have the advantage of me, sir," Jim said, borrowing Bones's phrase. "I don't know your name."

"Gurrhim tr'Siedhri, they call me."

Aha, Jim thought, for that was a name he had heard in passing from Ael. The dossier on him would make interesting rereading, later, in view of this meeting. He looked thoughtfully at the praetor's uniform. "Space services, perhaps?"

"Only long ago," tr'Siedhri said, "when they were differently constituted than they are now." Was that a breath of anger behind the nostalgia? "Now I am just a farmer."

Jim had to grin at that. "With all due respect, sir, I don't think it was talk about farm subsidies that brought you here."

Tr'Siedhri's eyes widened, and he produced that roaring laugh again. Heads turned around the room, and astonished eyes were fixed on them from here and there. Jim, looking past tr'Siedhri for a second, caught a glance from the t'Illialhlae woman. For once she had forgotten to keep her face still. Her glance at tr'Siedhri's back suggested she would like to see some edged implement buried in it—deep. "Why, here's fine news," said tr'Siedhri, "that you know our local business, *my* local business, so well. The Praetorate must after all be as riddled with spies as they've been claiming. Indeed the odds are short that there's anyone here who's not a spy of some kind."

The phrase "guilty as charged," used as a joke, occurred to Jim, but he decided it would be unwise to use it at the moment. "There must be *someone* normal here," he said instead.

"*Au,* the odds are still short," said tr'Siedhri. "Has anyone here *not* in the military ever held an honest job? No, it's just me, I fear, and little what's-her-name there, the housekeeper-as-was: Arrhae i-Khellian as she is now."

"Meaning that she 'was' something else?"

"Perspicacious," Gurrhim said. "But we won't speak of it. No, she's noble now, that's all that counts. They can't take that from her, not even if they kill her. Once a senator in ch'Rihan, always one—while you breathe, anyway."

"Breath," Spock said from behind the captain, "can be as precious a commodity for a senator, then, as votes?"

The praetor looked at Spock with another of those what-a-shiny-bug expressions. "Now here's a wonder," he said, "for who would have thought a Vulcan had any tittle of wit about him? But you too are slightly out of the ordinary as we reckon things. Votes, yes, Commander. The Senate depends on them. On our level of the House, we're praetor-blood as soon as we're born. A sad state of affairs. No need or reason to prove oneself worthy of the position . . . just heredity on your side, and that as fickle and unpredictable an ally as it is for everyone else. Time passes, inbreeding sets in, the vigor of noble old houses runs out of their descendants like blood from a slit vein . . ." He shook his head. "Nothing is as it was when we were young."

It was a complaint Jim had heard often enough before, but rarely with such a clear sense that the person voicing it was grandstanding, and to some purpose. He wondered what the purpose might be, for this man, who as he understood it had a fearsome reputation as a warrior in the ground forces when he was young, and later made the difficult transition to the Fleet with distinction, reaching Ael's rank before being called to the Praetorate and resigning all but a reserve commission. "Time, then, for the Elements to move toward reunion?" he asked.

The look tr'Siedhri gave Jim was amusing. "Not just yet," he said. "A few things to do before then . . . about which we will no doubt be speaking shortly."

"Not 'we,' I think," Jim said. "I am far less senior than some of the people here, Praetor. One of our poets better described my present role, I fear: 'They also serve who only stand and wait.' "

A small smile, a subdued expression, was the response, and it looked odd on this man, who seemed constructed for the big gesture and the exercise of power on a large scale. "Somehow," Gurrhim tr'Siedhri said, "I do not think you will be kept waiting long."

He lifted his glass. "Live well," he said, and tossed the ale back in one gulp. Jim blinked.

The praetor assumed a thoughtful expression. "Not a bad week, that," he said, and picked up the decanter. "May I top you up?"

Jim let him do it, aware of Spock's look resting on him and on the glass, and considered that prolonging this exchange would probably be worth the headache later. Anyway, McCoy could always slip him something to detoxify him a little; if anyone knew how to treat a Romulan ale overdose, considering recent history, it was McCoy.

"I should ask my friend to join me," Jim said, attempting to put off for a few seconds at least the prospect of doing to this glassful what tr'Siedhri had just done.

"Oh," tr'Siedhri said, "surely a Vulcan would not—"

"Surely," Spock said, "not."

"It was my other friend I was looking for," Jim said, turning away a little desperately. He was just going to have to drink the stuff down; there was no way out of it.

"Indeed?" tr'Siedhri said, looking past Jim.

Jim turned and saw McCoy. And someone else.

The doctor was not ten meters away, looking absently at the stars through the nearby wall. In front of him, making her way from one group of Romulans toward another, as calm and unconcerned as a cloud passing in front of the moon, a handsome, dark-haired Rihannsu woman passed him by in a drift of robes that shimmered like midnight silk. The long, dark, delicate scarf trailing sashwise over her shoulder and floating gently behind her now slipped lazily down her back and whispered to the shining white floor, pooling there as still as a shadow gone truant.

"Our other 'normal' one," tr'Siedhri said, too softly for anyone but Jim to hear.

McCoy heard the susurrus of the falling scarf, reacted with slight surprise, bent down, and picked it up. He strolled after her, and the sound of his footsteps brought her around.

"Sorry, ma'am," McCoy said, "you dropped this."

All this was happening, relatively speaking, away at the edge of things, but Jim, stealing a glance around the room, saw that some other eyes were now turned that way. One tall, thin woman by the door, in a long, relatively simple dark robe that would have passed for a very stylish evening dress in Earth society at the moment, was watching Senator i-Khellian very closely from behind a small knot of Rihannsu who were talking energetically about something else, oblivious to McCoy and the senator.

McCoy slipped the delicate silk through his hands once and then presented it to the lady, as if it were more a weapon than an ornament of dress. The senator looked quizzically from it to McCoy, and her expression took on an air of faint distaste as she looked him up and down. "It is not as if I don't have enough of them to be able to afford to lose one now and then," she said to him, very coolly, "and do not need to ask *you* to bring them back to me. Indeed, the last time we met you were more eager to throttle me than to be of any assistance. This is a pleasant change. May it be the herald of other unexpected civilities."

She reached out and took the scarf from him, draping it over one forearm and giving him a nod of dismissal. McCoy's bow was exactly that of a Southern gentleman being correctly polite to a lady who is being very correct with him. "At your service, ma'am," he said, and waited for her to turn away before doing so himself.

Off she went in her cloud of dark silk, and McCoy turned back toward the buffet table, seeing Jim and Spock there, and their sudden companion. He ambled over toward them, nodded to the praetor, and picked up a glass. "Captain," he said, "Mr. Spock."

"And so this is the other criminal," said tr'Siedhri mildly. "Now my evening is complete, at least unless t'Rllaillieu should put in an appearance. Gentlemen, live well." He raised his glass and drained it again.

Jim did the same, only hoping that this time his eyes wouldn't water. As usual, the hope was in vain.

"Doctor?" said the praetor, as McCoy filled his own glass.

"Here's mud in your eye, sir," McCoy said, and

97

knocked his straight back without having to be coached. A moment later he took a long breath and said, "You people are masochists."

"*Au*, no. Sadism, more usually, is our people's vice," said the praetor. "This is merely self-abuse. Gentlemen."

He gave the three of them just the slightest bow and went off toward the middle of the room, where various Rihannsu were talking quietly with Ambassador Fox. Jim glanced around and could see nothing of the tall woman who had been watching Senator i-Khellian; everyone else seemed to be looking everywhere else.

McCoy, meanwhile, was watching him with some slight concern. "You," he said, "are going to have a head on you the size of a Rigelian's in about an hour if you don't get back to the ship and have a dose of Old Doc McCoy's Famous Patent Nostrum for Overindulgence by the Diplomatically Minded."

"Believe me, Bones, it was on my mind," Jim said with feeling, for his eyeballs were starting to feel as if they were vibrating slightly in his head. "Let's go do it now."

"Not at all," McCoy said. "Rude to leave the party so soon. Give it half an hour or so, then you two go down to sickbay. I'll follow."

Spock put an eyebrow up. "The doctor is merely attempting to be left alone with the buffet. Or to run a covert physical on me a month early."

"You just keep believing that, Mr. Spock,"

McCoy said. "And as for the illicit pleasures of the table, which you are so far above, *I* saw what you were doing to that *plomeek* dip. Don't try to deny it."

They strolled off under the stars.

Half an hour later Jim and Spock were in sickbay, waiting impatiently. McCoy came in about ten minutes after they arrived, having stopped at his quarters to get rid of his dress uniform. "Damn thing's like being in traction," he said as he came through the doors. "Don't know why the surgeon general's office hasn't challenged the dress uniform on humanitarian grounds before now. Here."

He put out his hand to Spock, who held out a hand, slightly startled. McCoy dropped two tiny data chips into it. "They were stuck to her scarf, under the roll of the hemming. Almost missed them."

"Someone was watching her make the pass," Jim said. "Tall, dark-haired woman, black robes."

"Green eyes? Kind of a high coloration for a Romulan?" McCoy said. "Uh-oh. I think I may know that one. She must have been keeping away from me, or I would have spotted her for sure. She's Intelligence, Jim."

"Wonderful," Jim said. "Spock?"

The Vulcan was looking closely at the chips. "It is one of the high-density solid media," he said, "but not the newest. I will take them up to the bridge and see what they contain."

"I think I have a good guess," Jim said.

"Tried them in the reader in my quarters," McCoy said. "Both of them were gibberish."

"They will not be for long," Spock said. "Captain, if you will excuse me . . ." He headed out.

"Bones," Jim said, trying not to sound too plaintive, "there's a little man in my head rehearsing the percussion line for the 'Anvil Chorus.' Could you please . . ."

"Yeah, me too, just keep your tunic on." McCoy sat down behind his desk and began rummaging through it for a particular hypospray. He glanced up. "Jim," he said, "I'm kind of worried about Terise. Her cover was never meant to stand this kind of scrutiny."

"It withstood enough scrutiny to allow her to be elevated to the Senate, Bones . . ."

"In a hurried way," McCoy said, finding the hypo he wanted and getting up, "and with a lot of emotional overreaction going on in the upper levels of the government at that point, and the need to make a hero out of somebody, yes. But now there's going to be time for more detailed investigation. Both back on ch'Rihan and on the ship that brought her here, which has to be crawling with intelligence operatives. Every word she says is going to be scrutinized." He slid open one of his meds cabinets and started going through it. "And she's here in the first place, you can bet, because someone high up in the government has decided to use her to find out what someone else high up in the government is doing during these talks. No matter what she says or does, she's going to be in danger."

"She's a very intelligent young woman, if what

you told us is true," Jim said. "We're going to have to assume that she's capable of taking care of herself."

"She's more than half Rihannsu, by choice," McCoy muttered as he came up with the vial he wanted. "I'm just hoping that's going to be enough. She's swimming with the sharks for real at the moment, and there's nothing we can do to help."

"Meanwhile," Jim said, "Spock'll see what he can make of what she gave you."

"Yeah, well, what surprises me is that there should be two of those things. One I can understand. The second one is—what? An afterthought? A revision?"

"We'll know pretty soon. *Ow!*"

"Sorry, I have to do this bolus. Timed release won't help with what you drank." McCoy reversed the hypo and gave himself a spray in the arm. "*Ow!* Lord, that smarts."

"Crybaby."

"Now sit down," McCoy said. "Even Spock isn't going to be able to decode those chips in five minutes." He went over to the food slot and had it produce a pitcher of cold water and a couple of glasses. "And then tell me what that praetor said to you . . ."

101

Chapter Eight

EISN WAS just risen, and so was tr'Anierh when he heard the flitter landing outside his study and sighed. He was barely dressed and had only just had morning-draft, and here the man was already. "Who would be a praetor of the Empire?" he muttered. "All my influence and I can't even keep one of my peers out of my house until I've broken fast . . ."

He heard the door open, and the poor opener's faint protest. Down the hall he could hear Urellh pounding his way, noisy as a herd of *hlai*. Then the study door flew open, and in Urellh came bustling, all good cheer, actually rubbing his hands together. *Why does he never storm into Arhm'n's house this way?* tr'Anierh thought wearily. *Or perhaps he does, and I am merely his second stop today. Oh, happy Arhm'n, to be rid of him already . . .*

"The earliest reports have come back," Urellh said. "Matters are going well."

Tr'Anierh sat down again behind the desk as he watched Urellh pace up and down the room. The man was unable to sit still when he was excited; it was astonishing that he had been able to keep people from knowing what he was thinking when he was still in the Senate. *Except that most of the senators of his time were as dim as he,* tr'Anierh thought. "So what have you heard?"

"In the initial meeting they glossed over the attack at 15 Trianguli," Urellh said. "It was not without mention, of course, but they are so nervous as to the result of the negotiations that they have not put nearly as much weight on it as they might have. It goes very well indeed."

"Was the woman there?" said tr'Anierh, moving over to the bookshelves to start putting away the volumes he had been using the night before.

"No, she had been sent off somewhere out of the way," said Urellh, producing his first frown of the morning. "More's the pity. But she is not far, our people there think. They have begun remote sensor sweeps to locate her ship."

Tr'Anierh nodded. "I would not hope for too much success too quickly in that regard," he said, "but we will see what the scans reveal. They may become incautious of her while they try to prolong the talks to see what else they can discover about our situation."

"They will have just been given more to chew on than they will like," Urellh said, "and their minds should be more on others' troubles than on ours." He looked abnormally pleased.

That by itself bothered tr'Anierh, for he had recently come into rather more information than he wanted about some of Urellh's doings and had been puzzling over what to do with it. "Well," he said, "that is as well. We would not want them paying too much attention to our own preparations just now."

"They would be paying less attention still had those seven ships not been where they were not wanted," Urellh said. But he said it with much less venom than tr'Anierh would have expected. "However, it turns out that that ill-thought-out venture has perhaps done us a favor. There were folk aboard a few of those ships who might have done us a disservice had they returned." He was frowning now. "The less comfortable and aggressive some elements of the other power blocs in the Senate feel at the moment, the better I like it."

Tr'Anierh took a long breath. "I have been meaning to talk to you about this," tr'Anierh said, "and this is probably as good a time as any." He had been thinking of how to phrase this for some days; now he threw all those ideas away as useless temporizing. "As regards those disturbances on the outworlds . . ."

Urellh's frown got more threatening. "They are unimportant. A seasonal manifestation."

"I am not so sure of that," tr'Anierh said. "Urellh, I have seen clearly enough how Intelligence has been trying to manage this business, and the tactic is not working. I was willing enough to give it a chance to produce a positive result, but it has not done so. We should not be hunting those people down. The more Intelligence does so, the more foolish they look, especially when those they are hunting escape them and spread the word. And if our people in the outworlds are indeed growing dissatisfied with our rule, we should be working to find out why, and to put the problem right."

Urellh looked at him as if he had grown another head. "What should be done," he said, "is what *is* being done. They are being told what we require of them, and how to obey. If they do not obey, the results will be predictable. That predictability is what keeps them in order—"

"It is *not* keeping them in order," tr'Anierh said, turning on Urellh with a suddenness that actually made the man take a step backward. "I have other sources of news than those you see fit to allow around you, Urellh. A thousand dead on Jullheh three days ago in the rioting; the government buildings set alight on Saulnrih, and half the state's spacecraft there destroyed or stolen in a night. This is a new definition of *order!* The men and women in those seven ships had friends, and now they are stirring up others on their behalf."

Urellh glared at him. "That," he said, "is your problem to deal with, of your making, not mine. If I were of a suspicious turn of mind, I would think perhaps you sent those people into harm's way specifically to produce this result."

Tr'Anierh's face went hard as he took a couple of steps toward the other. "You would think hard before you made that claim as a certainty," he said softly, "for it would be the Park for you then, for certain. I am one of the Three, Urellh, whether you like the fact or not, whether you think the number too large or not. You had best study to resign yourself more completely to that fact." Urellh's face closed over as if he did not care, and he held his ground, but tr'Anierh was not fooled. "And as for your earlier accusations, I have only one thing to say. What about Eilhaunn, Urellh? How was it that the Klingons happened on *that* world at just such a time? Apparently knowing everything about where its defenses were—and what defenses it had?"

Urellh did not even have the grace to look embarrassed. "I know well enough that one of your creatures was responsible for that. Where does that leave you now with the Elements, after such behavior toward 'My people, whom I rule'?" There was no use trying to contain his scorn anymore. "Driven off as slaves now, sold to Klingon worlds, into lives of abuse and scorn, if lives they have at all! How have you protected *them?*"

"If it was not that world," said Urellh, "it would soon enough have been another. The Klingons were coming *anyway,* tr'Anierh! They would have struck deeper into our spaces, and found richer prey, richer worlds, ones more important to us, had the beasts not had a bone thrown them—something to satisfy their own command, something that would not affect our own security too deeply. Now they are stripping Eilhaunn, yes, but little enough they'll find for their pains. No industry to speak of, nothing of worth but slaves—and a long way to come for just those! *That* they will notice. They will think again before their next raid, for such poor payment. And they have shown their side of the board, in doing so. Now the Federation are looking their way, when once they had been concentrating wholly on us. That will cool their ale for them. No, we have lost a few lives, and gained many. And gained time, which is more precious than lives right now, for even though we seem to have acquired an early advantage in the talks, the game is still delicately balanced—"

Tr'Anierh looked at Urellh through his carefully suppressed distaste and anger and thought, *The 'package.' Where is it now? More: who does know where it is?* It was something he dared not ask about directly. To show interest at all would be to show his own side of the board, and where his counters lay. "I am still not sure I care for the physical circumstances," he said. "The Lalairu cannot be trusted not to interfere, and the Federation has begun to move much more significant assets into that area, as we know. Those six ships all by themselves—"

"Are enough to keep the Federation and the Starfleet people busy for the moment," Urellh said lightly, having apparently regained his composure. "Too busy to see the seventh that passes, if all goes well. If it does . . . then all our problems will be over, quite soon."

Tr'Anierh nodded, trying to look casual about it, trying to look as if the momentary unease had blown past him now. "Well," he said, "then all the trouble and disruption will have been worth something after all. And once it finally happens, the outworlds will fall into line quickly enough. The traitress's allies will be either destroyed or powerless, and the Klingons will swiftly enough learn to lie quiet lest they receive such a package themselves."

"I thought you would see sense eventually," Urellh said. Tr'Anierh held his face still until Urellh turned, for even now the man had no sense of his own arrogance and how transparent it was. "We have an early session today . . ." He was already halfway to the door.

"I know. I will be there."

Urellh went out without closing the door, as usual. Softly tr'Anierh crossed to it, shut it, and began to walk slowly toward the windows again, looking out at the expanse of reinforced pavement, with flitters and small courier craft parked on it, that ran up against the distant wall.

He is too intent on his own vision, tr'Anierh thought, *to see or allow the validity of any other. I wish he were merely mad; he might be turned from this course if he were. But he is all too sane.*

Now all that remains to be seen is whether I can make Arhm'n aware of the danger, and get him to turn my way rather than Urellh's.

And there was the other image, the image of the destruction of whole worlds. That was on his mind more or less constantly now, coming between him and his sleep and making the light of Eisn and the very greenness of the sky look uncertain in his eyes.

Tr'Anierh shivered. *Even the news of this thing,* tr'Anierh thought, *should be enough to strike fear into them. Knowing we have such a device, the Federation would not then dare move against us. We would have leisure enough to restore order in our own good time.*

But one way or another . . . they must know about it.

Tr'Anierh looked around the comfortable room, the shelves of books, almost properly organized now, the beautiful table with its delicate inlay over which he idly brushed his fingers. He thought of what lay outside that door, these windows—people and machines and wealth, the accessories of power, hard-earned over many years, all marshaled and ready to do his bidding. All he had to do to stay where he was, to keep what was his, was keep silent.

Let matters take their course. Do nothing. Nothing would happen to him. He was, after all, one of the Three.

Yet . . .

Are there things worth giving up all this for? There had seemed to be, when he was younger. Was that simply a stage that he had grown out of? He would have thought so. But now old doubts and fears that tr'Anierh had not felt for years were assailing him, and, having long ago given up the discipline of struggling with them every day, he was losing this struggle now.

The inlay in the table caught his eye again as his fingers brushed it, that one long stanza from "The Song of the Sun":

I am They; I am the light of their shining:
save by me, how shall you see and behold
Them?
How shall anything else be seen
save by the light of Their burning?
How shall the shapes of things be known
except that Truth burning give light thereto:
how shall reality be disclosed
without Them burning Themselves away?
Fused, the atom dies, yet by its dying we see,
Day by day, as the light
boils up from the depths of the starheart:
if the Elements for your sake
so burn themselves to nothing,
how much more you for each other?
How are you less than They?

He turned, looked out at the lawn. The sound of Urellh's departing flitter had almost faded to nothing against the normal morning city sounds. Things grew very quiet, very still, as tr'Anierh looked out into the burgeoning day, at Eisn's amber sunlight striking in sideways and casting long shadows from the trees that surrounded the compound. The shadows, to his dismay, looked more real than the light; the light looked temporary, endangered, ephemeral.

Tr'Anierh turned and headed quickly out of the room.

* * *

110

Aboard the *Enterprise,* Spock had returned to sickbay, not in a matter of minutes, but after nearly an hour. He dropped a small data solid on the desk. Jim picked it up and turned it over in his hands. "The cryptography," Spock said, "decoded correctly, but I wished to take some extra time to be sure of the encoded 'signatures' associated with the material." He looked grave.

"And?" Jim said.

"They were both genuine. But the material is, to put it mildly, explosive. It comes in two different sets, as you will have gathered from the two chips. One set of data purports to be from another Federation operative on ch'Rihan, who I fear we may assume has come to what the doctor would doubtless describe as 'a bad end.' "

"And just how can we assume that?" McCoy asked.

"Because I have run a syntactic and stylistic analysis on that entire set of data, Doctor," Spock said. "Even within a single short letter or message, each unique writer has specific telltales, stylistic tendencies from sentence structure to punctuation, which can serve as a guide to the genuineness of the text as a whole. In this case, there are alterations to the operative's text, in a style that differs quantifiably, to no less than an eighty-four percent certainty, from its main body. The immediate suggestion, to my mind at least, is that the material was taken from this operative under, shall we say, less than optimum circumstances, and altered afterward so that we should accept it as genuine. Mostly the data has to

111

do with troop and ship movements in the parts of Romulan space closest to the Neutral Zone, and if my conjectures as to the purposes of those who altered it are correct, we are meant to believe that the Rihannsu are not preparing for any major offensive, or rather not one against us, but for a 'police action' against rebellious elements within the Imperium."

"The intel people are going to want to make up their own minds about that," Jim said.

"Yes, Captain. But I would guess that their analysis will not be very different from mine." Spock folded his arms and leaned back. "The other set of data—" He looked at McCoy. "Doctor, I have read Lieutenant Haleakala-LoBrutto's initial report on her stay on ch'Rihan, but you have had more recent contact with her. I would appreciate your input as to whether you note stylistic changes in the content. I do not, however."

"I'll look at it right away, Spock. But what's the story?"

"It is a remarkable one." Spock's expression, to Jim's eye at least, got much graver. "There would seem to be some truth in the first data set's report of rebellion among the Romulan Empire's worlds. There is indeed such rebellion. But it is far worse than we have expected. The commander has not overstated the case in the slightest; possibly she has understated it, and the first report may have acknowledged rebellion in the first place because it has become impracticable to continue disguising or suppressing the truth. Various of the outermost worlds, which normally have a somewhat less stringent level of government imposed on them by the Senate and Praetorate—for the good reason that it is logistically more difficult to exert such control over great distances—are beginning to move to assert what on Earth once would have been called UDI . . ."

"Unilateral declarations of independence," Jim said softly.

"Yes, Captain. The rebellious factions have correctly assessed the central government's position. It is now too busy handling internal problems closer to home, similar rebellions and disaffections, and most lately the matter of the commander and the lost Sword, to effectively crack down on the worlds farthest away. According to the news which Lieutenant LoBrutto has been given to pass on to us, these more distant colony worlds have become themselves disaffected over recent years by the Rihannsu government's decision to withdraw its protection from them while continuing to demand ever higher taxes and conscription. And on some of the most distant worlds, where the families who settled were those of the engineers and pilots of the old-generation ships, the disaffection is strongest and is now erupting into the open. On those worlds, so Lieutenant LoBrutto says she has been told, the leaders of the movement—if that is the word for it, its organization being loose—have spent years amassing the capital, resources, and manpower to secretly begun building great ships again."

"Secretly?" Jim said. "That must take some doing, with their bureaucracy. But what kind of 'great ships'?"

McCoy was already shaking his head. "Knowing those people," he said, "knowing what I heard about the ship-clans while I was there—they won't just be generation ships, this time. They'll be multipurpose . . ."

"Warships, then," Jim said.

Spock nodded. "The outworlds are now intent on their freedom. Their people would largely prefer to remain Rihannsu. But as such, they are also pragmatists, and they know the present government will not let them go without a fight. They are preparing to fight for their worlds' freedom, and if they cannot achieve this, they intend to lead their people out into the long night again, and never return."

Jim swallowed. It was nothing less than the beginning of the disintegration of an empire that Spock was discussing so calmly, but Jim knew all too well from history that where one empire fell, another would rush in to fill the vacuum unless something happened to stop the process.

"Several of the great ships are complete already, apparently," Spock said. "They have been built in orbit and concealed in the asteroid belts of several of the colony worlds where the Rihannsu government's surveillance is poorest. Several more will be ready soon. And meanwhile, as a result of this—for the leading minds in the movement have seen to it that the news has seeped out—thousands of Rihannsu have begun demonstrating in the cities of the outworlds.And there has been considerable civil disorder associated with the demonstrations, along with destruction or theft of government property. This is information which has apparently been suppressed by the authorities on ch'Rihan until now. Lieutenant LoBrutto says that they have had less success suppressing the larger-scale demonstrations on ch'Havran, but the government continues to attempt to deny what is going on, or to pretend that it is unimportant. Some of the Praetorate know the truth, and have spoken it, but they are not popular."

Jim thought of the great bear of a man who had towered over him, looking at him so curiously, so speculatively. He wondered if he now understood something of the reason why. "Spock," he said, "doesn't Gurrhim tr'Siedhri have ship-clan connections?"

"Indeed he does, Captain. Normally someone with such close ties would not survive long in the Praetorship, but his hereditary rights to the title cannot be denied, and he wields considerable power because of extensive land holdings on both ch'Rihan and ch'Havran, but more so on the latter world, which also has ship-clan ties of its own which ch'Rihan does not. He would be seen by the other praetors, particularly by the 'ruling' three, as at least potentially subversive, and a danger to them, but so far they have not found a way to reduce his 'dangerousness.' "

"Short of killing him," McCoy said, "which is something that does happen to you sometimes in Rihannsu politics." He folded his arms, leaned back.

Diane Duane

"I'd watch how I drank, if I were him, and who poured it out of what bottle."

"And Ael . . ." Jim said.

"Ael," Spock said. "There are apparently many among the ship-clans who see her as someone they can use as a banner, a rallying point."

"Knowing the commander," McCoy said, "I'm not sure who would be using whom, exactly."

"She would certainly be willing to use this kind of force if it was offered to her in alliance," Jim said. "But is it really enough, do they really have the resources, to unseat an empire? Spock?"

"The lieutenant's data has numerous lacunae," Spock said. "The data apparently came to her in some haste, and she passed it on the same way to her superiors in Starfleet Intelligence—whom it will only now be reaching. But the kind of uprising presently taking place is unprecedented in the history of the Imperium. Whatever the final outcome, the Romulan Star Empire as we have known it is about to change forever."

"This is news we've got to get to Ambassador Fox," Jim said, getting up. "He would get it from Intel himself, anyway, but not as quickly. Talk about timely . . ."

"It is," McCoy said. "In the case of the first set of information, of course, the timeliness is obviously planned."

"Yes. Now we've got to figure out which way they think we're going to jump as a result of it." He headed out. "Spock? Let's go see if the ambassador's available."

* * *

He wasn't, but this hardly came as a surprise to Jim, considering what the events of the next day were going to entail. All they could do was leave a copy of the information and a précis with Fox's assistant at his office aboard *Speedwell,* and head back to *Enterprise* to wait for the proceedings to commence. Jim went to bed and dreamed uneasily of things exploding in the darkness, and of the light of the nearby star suddenly beginning to balloon out at him in the unnerving way it had at 15 Tri.

He was up earlier than necessary and found Spock already on the bridge. "Did you sleep at all last night?" Jim said.

"No more than need required," Spock said, rather absently, as he was looking down his scanner at the moment. "There have been other matters in need of my attention."

Jim sat down at the helm and rubbed his face. "Anything interesting?"

Spock straightened up and stepped down toward the center seat, where he stood looking at the viewscreen. It was showing *Mascrar* and not much else, which was no particular surprise, considering the thing's size. "The Romulan vessels," he said, "have been evincing a considerable amount of scan activity since they arrived."

Jim made a face. "Looking for Ael, I bet."

"It would seem a logical conclusion," Spock said. "Though one might reasonably expect them to be more circumspect about it."

Sulu looked over his shoulder. "Maybe they think

117

there's no point in trying to hide it at all," he said, "since the level of surveillance around them is going to be so high anyway, and also it's what everyone would *expect* them to be doing."

Spock let out what would have sounded like a sigh of mild frustration in a human. "It can often be difficult to tell what a Romulan is thinking," he said, "even in mind-meld. Or rather, what he means by what he is thinking." He kept gazing at *Mascrar* as if attempting to see through it into the Romulan ships and possibly into their crews' brains.

"Well, keep an eye on them," Jim said and stretched. Behind him the turbolift doors opened, and Lieutenant Uhura came in. "You're on shift early, Lieutenant."

She gave him a smile that suggested she knew his reason for having jumped his own on-shift time by an hour or so. "If I've got to be on tenterhooks about what's going on over there, sir," Uhura said, "I may as well be that way up here as at breakfast. And up here I won't drink so much coffee."

Jim gave her an ironic look as Spock went back up to his station. "Well, let me give you something to do besides contemplate your blood caffeine level, then. Spock, those new comm ciphers are in place, aren't they?"

"The ones for use at the present time," Spock said, "yes, Captain."

"Good. Uhura, are you certain that they're properly implemented?"

"I ran them through a full test cycle last night," Uhura said. "Everything seemed fine."

"Good. Then hail *Ortisei* for me, would you? I wouldn't mind a word with Captain Gutierrez."

"Yes, Captain."

Jim sat and watched *Mascrar* rotating gently for a few moments. *It's not like we wouldn't have suspected they'd be looking for her,* he thought. *They obviously want advance notice of her coming into range. The only question is, What use of that information are they preparing to make? They wouldn't dare try to attack her under all our noses. They're seriously outgunned . . .*

. . . aren't they?

"*Ortisei* is answering, Captain," said Uhura.

"On screen," Jim said.

Mascrar disappeared, to be replaced by the bridge of another starship of *Enterprise*'s class. In its center seat sat a big, broad-shouldered man with broad, open features and very cool eyes; longish auburn hair was neatly bound back while he was in uniform. "Afterburner," Jim said, "how are things?"

Captain Harold Gutierrez sat back in the center seat, stretched his arms out in front of him with the fingers interlaced, and cracked his knuckles. "Dead quiet at the moment," he said, "but in this neighborhood you'd expect that. How're things closer in to the primary?"

"Heating up," Jim said. "I won't spoil any surprises for you, but you should expect a package from

Fox and the team this morning. Some interesting reading in there."

"I just bet." Gutierrez made a slightly sour face, and Jim controlled the urge to smile. This was another of the commanders in Starfleet who had acquired something of a reputation for quick action in a crisis, and a gift for finding a crisis to exploit, so much so that Jim could entirely understand why Fleet hadn't wanted him here on site with both Helgasdottir and Danilov: fighting would have broken out spontaneously, as unavoidable as the results when you mix nitric acid and glycerin. "So when do the fireworks start?"

"They've already started, I'm told. Major formal 'representations' will be made shortly, but both sides already know what these are, apparently. What we're going to be expecting is reactions to the representations. Which is why I thought I'd call."

"So I suspected. No, everything's fine here, Jim," Gutierrez said. "All's quiet on *Bloodwing.* I spoke to Commander t'Rllaillieu about half an hour ago, in fact."

"And?"

"No problems," Gutierrez said, "except that I think she'd dearly love to present herself right in front of her people's noses to see how far out of joint they get."

"I can imagine. Well, don't let it happen without Danilov saying the word," Jim said, "or we're all going to be in the soup together. Meanwhile, how's the new baby?" *Ortisei* was Harry's second command; *Raksha* had been decommissioned out from under him because of advancing age and a warp engine that kept malfunctioning when no one could figure out why.

"She's a honey," Harry said. "The rough edges are pretty much sanded off now. My chief engineer thinks we can start doing some customizing now."

"Uh-oh," Jim said. "Keep a close eye on her. You never know what they're going to install down there when you're not looking."

Harry snorted. "As if I get a say. But she and the commander were swapping busted-engine stories, and—"

Jim shook his head, smiling. "Trouble already. Well, look, Harry, while you're keeping an eye on the two of them, don't neglect your sensors to the outward. My science officer tells me that certain ships not a million kilometers from here are doing a lot of scanning."

"Theoretically we should be well out of range," Harry said, "but I'll have Mr. Mitchelson peel a few extra of his eyes and see if he notices anything unusual. It's not like there haven't been occasional breakthroughs in scanning technology in the last five or ten years."

"Good. Call and let us know if you find anything of interest. And give my best to the commander when you speak."

"Will do, Jim. *Ortisei* out."

The screen flickered, then went back to its view of *Mascrar.*

Uhura had one hand to the transdator in her ear. She turned toward Jim and said, "Captain, the for-

mal opening proceedings are about to start. Mr.
Freeman has rigged the big holo display down in rec
for viewing, but I imagine there'll be a lot of off-
duty people watching down there, and it might get
crowded. Shall I put it up on the screen for you
here?"

"Nothing else to watch but the scenery," Jim said.
"Please do."

The room to which the viewscreen cut was another of those with floor-to-ceiling windows, all
looking out into space—another room in the "city
hall" spire of *Mascrar*—but this one contained nothing else but the biggest circular table Jim had ever
seen, easily thirty meters across. More properly, it
was not a circle, but a ring, empty in the center so
that assistants could come and go with padds and paperwork and so forth. On one side of it were the Rihannsu, nearly fifty of them all told, the last of them
seating themselves now. Opposite them the Federation delegation sat, nearly as many—if not exactly as
many, Jim thought. He let his eyes slide around to
the background of the view that the Lalairu camera
was giving them and caught a glimpse of Sam Cogley back there, and not too far from him, though well
separated from him by an empty "neutral" space, a
slender, handsome woman now dressed in dark
clothes much less formal than the ones she had been
wearing the previous evening. Arrhae i-Khellian. He
was very glad to see her there, looking untroubled—
though, heaven knew, appearances could be deceiv-

ing. At least she seemed to be in no immediate trouble with the dark-featured intelligence operative whom McCoy had reported was watching her. *Let's hope it stays that way.*

The opening comments from both sides went on for half an hour or so, from Ambassador Fox on the Federation side and Gurrhim tr'Siedhri on the other, before things started to heat up, and Jim watched it all, becoming increasingly concerned. The atmosphere in the room looked leisurely enough as the two elder statesmen went on in turn about mutual respect and past misunderstandings. But Jim could feel the tension as plainly as if he were sitting there in the middle of those people, all so busy looking statesmanlike, when Hloal t'Illialhlae stood up to read the official Rihannsu position paper. *They already know they're going to get an answer they won't like,* Jim thought, *and they're beginning to consider just what they're going to do about it.*

Hloal t'Illialhlae was reading the position paper from a padd on the table in front of her. Why she was reading it standing wasn't entirely clear to Jim. *Just that the gesture itself is threatening? Or because she looks more impressive that way? Or is there some other cultural thing?* But she was wearing just a shade of a smile, and the look of it troubled Jim obscurely. "We desire, as you do," she was saying now, "to bring an end to the unfortunate conflicts between our peoples which have troubled the tranquillity of our spaces and yours for a number of years, distracting all our attention from matters of more importance. The final resolution of these conflicts may most swiftly be brought about by the acknowledgment and implementation of the following four points. First: the abolition of the so-called Neutral Zone and the declaration by the Federation of what is true and known to be true, that these spaces have been, are, and will remain in perpetuity the territory of the Rihannsu Star Empire, and the surrender to our authority of all the surveillance facilities, known as monitoring outposts, in that zone of space. Second: the public acknowledgment by the Federation of previous thefts of vital technology and intellectual property from our territory, vessels, and citizens, including the cloaking device stolen from the vessel ChR 1675 *Memenda,* and certain research materials formerly located at Levaeri V before the unprovoked attack on and looting of that facility; and a public apology for those thefts, accompanied by an undertaking never to use or develop the technologies or materials acquired in those thefts. Third: the immediate return for trial of the woman Ael i-Mhiessan t'Rllaillieu, formerly a commander-general in the Space Forces of the Rihannsu Star Empire and self-acknowledged traitor to the Empire; though our government has chosen to relinquish any claim on the antiquated vessel that she stole, and has graciously chosen to commute to perpetual banishment the sentence of death passed on her crew, personages who have proved themselves unfit for further service in our military services by reason of allowing themselves to be duped by the aforesaid t'Rllaillieu and made accomplices in her crimes against the Empire. And fourth: the immediate return of the cultural artifact which the aforesaid t'Rllaillieu stole, variously known as the Fifth Sword of S'harien, the Sword of S'task, or the Sword in the Empty Chair."

She sat down again, looking most poisonously demure. Jim sat there listening to the little rustle of reaction going through the room, and for his own part was amazed by the tone of calm threat and absolute insolence. *You'd think they already had a big force sitting on the Moon, dictating terms, while they got ready to drop something large and nasty on the Earth.* "Huh," said McCoy's voice, ironic, from behind the center seat.

Jim glanced over his shoulder. "Didn't hear you come in."

"Nope. I see, though," Bones said, "that a couple of the pawns have been knocked off the board already."

Jim nodded. There had been no mention of the return of *Bloodwing* or her crew. "Somehow, though," Jim said, "I don't think Starfleet is going to agree to hand the Neutral Zone over to them."

McCoy shook his head. "No, or the Sunseed routines, either."

Jim nodded again. Fox was standing up to speak, now, and not bothering with a padd. "I thank the noble praetor for her clarification of the Imperium's intentions," he said, "and intend to respond in kind. Certainly much time and energy has been spent pursuing courses of action which have caused difficulty to both the Star Empire and the Federation, and any reasonable being would consider it prudent to seek to resolve these outstanding issues between us and move on into positions of greater interstellar security, always remembering that we are not the only two major powers to be reckoned with in the present scheme of things."

Did Gurrhim and a few of the other Romulans blink at that bit of frankness? Jim looked closely at them and couldn't be sure. "As regards the Star Empire's four points," Fox said, "first: any change in the status of the Neutral Zone would have to be taken after a period of extensive consultation with the various inhabited planets in the area and a thorough investigation into the various consequences of such a change in the status of the area. Needless to say, so major a change would require some while to implement properly, with an eye to guaranteeing the continued peace and security of the star systems in this area, and the logistics of the change would need careful coordination among the interested parties. Regardless, the Federation will give this proposal careful consideration and will reply in more detail in due course."

McCoy snorted softly. "As regards the second point," Fox went on, "the Federation fully understands the concern that unauthorized intrusions into Rihannsu space cause the Star Empire. The Federation has suffered various similar intrusions into its own space of late, and is well acquainted with the annoyance secondary to the loss of valuable equipment and personnel, as well as the loss of face which is invariably associated with such tragedies." *That* had an effect: Hloal t'Illialhlae turned a most astonishing jade color and stirred in her chair as if about to leap out of it. "However, the Federation has no desire to reopen old wounds at this time, or, for that matter, to inflame new ones, and is minded to let bygones be bygones in this regard. I am, however, empowered to say that the Federation will consider such gestures toward truth and reconciliation in tandem with the Rihannsu Star Empire's own consideration of such gestures, and stands ready to make a simultaneous public announcement at such a time as the Empire is prepared to do so in regards to its own previous incursions. Third—"

The hellish image of the chromosphere of 15 Trianguli rose up in front of Jim, and the memory of seven ships chasing *Enterprise* and *Bloodwing* around it and out into the cold again. His back itched as if the sweat were running down it all over again as they ran for their lives. "That's *it?*" Jim said. *"That's* all he's got to say about—"

"Shh," McCoy said.

"I can't *believe* this!"

"—as regards the former commander-general Ael i-Mhiessan t'Rllaillieu, the United Federation of Planets is presently engaged in discussions intended to clarify her legal position with regard to her presence and possible rights under law in Federation space. Until such clarification is available, I regret that no statement can be made regarding her disposition. **Additionally, and in regard** to your fourth point, since there is some uncertainty regarding her whereabouts, it is at this time difficult to say whether the artifact about which you are inquiring is actually in her possession or not. Needless to say, it is the Federation's wish that any artifact of cultural value should be restored to its proper place as soon as the facts of the case have been understood and evaluated by those most closely involved, and we would hope that such an evaluation could occur at the earliest possible date."

And Fox sat down.

Jim just sat there, speechless. The only satisfaction he got for the moment was that the Romulans were doing the same.

After a moment, Hloal t'Illialhlae leaned across the table and looked hard at Fox. "When," she said, "might we reasonably expect this 'legal clarification' to be forthcoming?"

"I expect it within thirty-six of our hours," Fox said promptly, "and I would hope your schedule allows you to remain here that long, so that whatever the nature of the clarification, we may then expedite further talks arising from it."

Jim wasn't entirely sure he liked the sound of that.

"We will return," said t'Illialhlae, "in thirty-six hours, then." She stood up, as did all her delegation. "But, Ambassador Fox, you must understand our position. If we do not achieve satisfaction on all four points by that time, the results will be unfortunate."

Fox and the people on the Federation side all stood up as well. "Intemperate action without the advice and consent of one's superiors is always unfortunate," Fox said. Jim raised his eyebrows at that, for it was astonishing how so cool and seemingly casual an utterance could seem suddenly edged with threat. "We look forward to meeting with you again, thirty-six hours from now."

The Romulans filed out, eldest first, as was their habit, though there was something of a clear space between Hloal t'Illialhlae and everyone else, as if not even her own people cared to get too close. Shortly the screen showed only an empty room, and Uhura killed that view, leaving Jim looking at the serenely rotating bulk of *Mascrar* again.

Sulu blew out a long breath but said nothing. Jim swung around in the center seat to look over at Spock, who was turning back to look down his scanner as if he had been watching nothing of more moment than one of Mr. Freeman's rechanneled ancient videos down in the rec room. Uhura just shook her head a little and then put her hand to her transdator, listening.

"That was the Ambassador's aide," she said. "There'll be a briefing for the negotiating team and the ships' captains in about eight hours. Apparently Fox expects the talks with the main body of Romulan negotiators and observers to resume again later this afternoon, regardless of what we just saw."

Jim nodded, trying to get a grip on himself and slowly finding it.

McCoy let out a long breath, looking at the screen again. "At least he stood up to tell them that last part."

"It does mean something, then . . ."

"You don't fight your enemy sitting down,"

McCoy said. "Challenges are always delivered standing, unless you so despise the enemy that you don't feel you need to do them that honor, or you foresee an outcome where you needn't have bothered to extend the courtesy, because they're not going to be alive long enough for it to matter." He shook his head. "At least Fox understands the nuances."

"I certainly hope he does," Jim said. "The good ambassador isn't without his occasional blind spot, as we've seen." The memory of the near disaster that had been triggered by Fox's actions when *Enterprise* had ferried him to Eminiar VII was all too vivid in Jim's mind. He was willing to cut the man some slack: while his actions on behalf of the Federation there had been somewhat ham-handed, there had never been any doubt but that his intentions had been good. But good intentions were not always enough. Fox's insistence on *Enterprise* remaining in the system even though the Eminians had warned her off resulted in the ship being declared "destroyed" in the virtual war between Eminiar and Vendikar. It was only smart action by Scotty, then in command while Jim, Spock, and the rest of the landing party were being held prisoner on the planet, that had kept the ship from really being destroyed, and had bought the landing party the time to escape, change the odds, and effectively end the war.

That had been a while ago, though. People did change and learn. Jim had heard of no further disasters with Fox's name attached to them. *And Starfleet must think he's the best we've got at the moment,*

Jim thought. He hoped with unusual fervor that they were right.

He also wondered what one who understood the nuances better than anyone on the Federation side was making of it all . . .

"Captain," Ael said, allowing herself to start to sound irritated, "you must not so misconstrue me. This is *not* a matter of whim, but one of personal honor, and as such cannot be deprioritized. Indeed, I had not thought your people went in much these days for instruments of torture, but I see I have yet much to learn." She leaned forward in her command chair and gave Captain Gutierrez, on the viewscreen, a fierce look. Behind her was a soft rustling of uniforms and creaking of chairs as a shift change took place—Aidoann and the day crew coming on—but it was happening much more quietly than usual. Ael's people were listening with an intensity that suggested they were very interested, or very amused, or both.

"Commander," said Captain Gutierrez, moving uncomfortably in his own center seat, "please, it's just a figure of speech. I simply mean that we cannot turn up in the neighborhood of *Mascrar* without security precautions first being in place."

"There are six Federation starships there, two of them most outrageously overweaponed, if I understand even the public specs for *Sempach* and *Speedwell*," Ael said, "not to mention *Mascrar*, which is closer in strength to a planetary-level defense installation. How much more security could you need?"

She shook her head at him as he started to speak. "Captain, my people have been foully maligned!" Ael said. "It is an act of dishonor for me to sit here and keep mum, as if fear or shame motivated me! *Mnhei'sahe* requires that I return with all due speed to defend my people's reputations as reasoning, thinking beings. Not to mention the reputation of *Bloodwing,* a vessel worthy of a better assessment than 'antiquated'!" She let the scorn show a little.

"Oh, come on, Commander. We have a saying: 'Sticks and stones may break my bones, but words will never hurt me.' "

She shook her head in mock wonder. "Such violence in idiom surprises me from the representative of a purportedly peaceful people."

"Commander, it's a *children's* saying. It means—"

"Elements protect me from your children, then!"

Aidoann, behind her, cleared her throat softly. Ael glanced at her and shook her head. It was a planned interruption, but it was not needed at the moment.

Gutierrez looked put out. "It means that just because they call your ship names, that's no reason to overreact—"

"Indeed? I seem to remember that Captain Kiurrk's crew once nearly precipitated a diplomatic incident because some Klingon called the *Enterprise* a 'garbage scow.' "

"That was different," Gutierrez said. "If the captain—"

"Sir," Ael said. "The insult that has been leveled at my crew is not one I can let slide. I swore to be their good lady and to lead them faithfully and well. Their long loyalty to me requires I take action to defend them. Even your culture, surely, supports the right to directly confront one's accusers when accusations so unbearable are made! Now, Captain, you must call the commodore, or whoever else you feel you must consult about this matter, and see to it that whatever 'security measures' need requires are put swiftly in place—for I will *not* linger here another two days while that slander on my crew lies smarting in my mind, and those who committed it sit about congratulating themselves. One standard day I give you. Then I will make my way back to the location of the talks . . . with you or without you. And we shall see what happens then."

Gutierrez swallowed again. Ael thought with secret amusement that she could almost hear him swallow, the only sound on her bridge except for the soft purr of the life-support systems and the occasional *beep* or *tck* of a touched control or closing circuit.

"Commander," Gutierrez said, "you know I can't permit that."

The temptation to say *And how will you stop me?* was strong, but would have been unwise: it would have made him start thinking too actively about ways to do so. "Perhaps you cannot," Ael said, "but a good way to see that it does not become an issue is to speak to the commodore immediately. We will talk again when you have done so."

Diane Duane

She glanced over at tr'Hrienteh and flicked the finger of one hand up the other wrist. Tr'Hrienteh killed the connection. "Answer no hails from *Ortisei* for the next four hours or so," Ael said, "and raise the shields. I will speak no more to Captain Gutierrez until he has better news for me."

Aidoann swung down from the engineering station, where she had been running some engine checks. *"Khre'Riov,"* she said, "you can't think that any of us take Hloal's mouth-wind at all seriously."

"Au, not at all," Ael said. "But Captain Gutierrez does not know that. Nor do I mean him to." Nonetheless she sat back in her hard command seat and smiled. "All the same, I find our good fortune hard to believe. Their arrogance has made them foolish, Aidoann. We lie here sinking in deep water, and they throw us a line, giving us an excuse to be right where we want to be."

"Always assuming, *khre'Riov,* that it was not their intent to play us so."

Ael cocked an eye up at Aidoann. "This cautious tone becomes you, cousin; you are growing into the habits of command. But the thought occurred to me some while ago." She leaned back, crossing her legs and making herself as comfortable as she could in that hard seat. "Yet I do not credit it. They are too far from remembering how true honor motivates action to use it effectively as a trap. When we do appear, and what must happen, happens, it will have been their own foolishness that brings it down on their heads. Meanwhile, we must prepare ourselves: we may have to move more quickly than in just one standard day. I must see tr'Keirianh immediately." She got up. "Call the engine room and tell him I am on my way. I want to see those new propulsion models, for my heart tells me that in some hours, we will need them."

In the neighborhood of RV Trianguli, aboard *Sempach,* the scheduled briefing between the negotiating team and the top-level officers of the starships on site had been going on for half an hour or so. Ambassador Fox had finished delivering the précis of the negotiations that had led to the morning's "public" session, and a shorter one of the afternoon's work. Now he pushed the padd away and sat back in his chair at the briefing-room table, as the stars slid slowly past the window and the great bulk of *Mascrar* began to slip into view.

"It's actually going relatively well," he said, "despite the apparent ultimatum we were offered. It's standard enough tactics in talks like this to go 'hard' after the opposing party gives you a 'soft' response to the initial proposals—or what are supposed to be the initial ones. You'll all have noticed that the initial Romulan official proposal was a lot milder than expected on the issues that really concern us, though more robust in other areas. The Neutral Zone, specifically."

From where he sat between Spock and McCoy, Jim looked up as sunlight reflected from *Mascrar* began to flood into the room. "It's the 'softness,' "

Jim said to Fox, "that is concerning me at the moment. I would have liked to see the incident at 15 Trianguli discussed in rather greater detail."

Danilov looked over at Fox, then at Jim. "That," he said, "is a matter which Starfleet Command has decided not to press any further, with a view to advancing other discussions considered more pertinent at the moment."

Spock glanced in Jim's direction. Jim folded his arms so that he wouldn't start drumming his fingers on the table. "Commodore," Jim said, "with all due respect, this does *not* strike me as a way for Starfleet to improve or augment the respect with which its ships are treated when they travel into debatable space."

"Captain," said Danilov, "I know what you're thinking. You were the one stuck in a tough place and getting shot at. But you got out of it with your skin intact, as you usually do—and now we have other fish to fry."

Oh no, Jim thought. He had always been warned of what happened when a ship started to become legendary for something. Soon it started to be taken for granted that the ship would always do what it had managed, sometimes by the skin of its teeth, to do until then.

"Commodore, I'm sorry, but I have to emphasize this," Jim said. "What if some other ship, not *Enterprise* with her admittedly laudable record for getting out of trouble, had happened into the situation we found waiting for us at 15 Tri? And had not come out of it? It would unquestionably have been a *casus belli*. But because we escaped, through good luck and bloody-mindedness, the subject is just going to be allowed to fall by the wayside?"

Danilov looked at Jim and said nothing. "They are going to draw certain inevitable conclusions from this," Jim said. "And the wrong ones. That we are so afraid of going to war that we will make considerable concessions to avoid it. Giving Romulans this idea is a major error. The location of the encounter is no accident, but the encounter itself is a message written in letters half a light-year high. They were not merely testing our preparedness in that part of space, but seeing whether we would call them on it. We didn't. We've apparently bent over backwards to let them weasel out of it! And now they have the answer they want. They've seen that they can commit a major breach of the treaty, an attack on a ship nominally under Federation protection, fairly deep in our space, and get away with it."

"Permission to speak freely," Danilov said softly, "granted."

Jim fell silent.

"Captain," Danilov said, "you're overstating the case. Fifty planets are not the same as one ship. Those worlds are populated by Federation citizens—"

"Was *Bloodwing* granted free passage through Federation space, or not?" Jim said. "Were her people given asylum here, or not?"

,Around the table, some of the most senior officers looked at one another uncomfortably. Jim knew why, for the legal position was still being "clarified" at the Federation High Council level, and no one wanted to commit themselves without having at least a clue of which way the Council would jump. *Politics!* Jim thought, and looked at Danilov. Danilov returned his gaze, his face not changing.

"The camel's nose is in the tent, gentlemen," Jim said. "And the rest of it is going to follow. I must protest the way the negotiations are going in the strongest possible terms."

He looked at Fox.

"It seems we're fated to be on the wrong side of these arguments, Captain," Fox said. "My instructions from the Federation High Council are very clear, and they give me little latitude for improvisation in some regards, no matter what my personal feelings on the subject might be."

There it was, as clear as his position would let him say it: *I don't approve either, but I have my job to do.* Jim breathed out.

"Ambassador," said Captain Helgasdottir, "allow me to say a word here."

All heads turned to her. Birga Helgasdottir pursed her lips and folded her hands together.

"I agree with Captain Kirk," she said. "If this matter of the incursion at 15 Trianguli is not pressed with the Romulans now, and vigorously, we are all going to suffer for it later."

Danilov gave Captain Helgasdottir a look not quite as annoyed as the one he had given Jim. "I'm sorry to find opinion so divided," he said, "when for the time being, the execution of policy must continue to go the way it's presently going. We must wait the forty or so hours left us, let this move of the game play itself out, and see how the Romulans react. There have been some early indications of a softening in their position; we'll see what further ones turn up tomorrow, after subspace messages have had time to make their way home to the Empire and back here again. But the whole situation is riding on a knife-edge at the moment, and if any evidence of divisions among us reaches the other side, it could wreck everything. I expect you all"—he glanced around the table—"to conduct yourselves accordingly."

Helgasdottir was wearing a tight look that suggested clearly enough to Jim how little she liked this, but she nodded. The other starship captains— the tall blond Centauri, Finn Winter of *Lake Champlain*, and the slender dark-maned Caitian, Hressth ssha-Aurrffesh of *Hemalat*—nodded too. They kept their faces neutral, but Jim got the strong feeling that neither of them felt any happier about this than he and Helgasdottir did. *They know,* Jim thought, *it could be* them *all alone out in the dark the next time . . .*

The meeting went on for a little while more, mostly dealing with administrative business and the movement of various supplies and resources among the gathered ships; it was unusual enough for so many Starfleet vessels to meet away from a starbase or between scheduled resupply or careening stops. Finally, Danilov stood up and said, "That's all for now, ladies and gentlemen. Dismissed." As the group rose with him, he glanced at Jim. "Captain Kirk, would you stay a moment?"

Jim stayed where he was; the room emptied.

When the door finally shut, Danilov sat down again. "Jim," he said, "I need a favor from you."

"Permission to speak freely?" Jim said.

"Granted."

Jim took a long breath, then let it out again. "Forget it," he said. "What is it you need, Dan?"

"I need you to send a message to the commander," he said, "telling her at all costs to stay where she is for the moment."

I wondered how long she was going to maintain her position. Now, is this one of her sudden hunches . . . or something more concrete? "What's the story at your end, Dan?" Jim said. "Not the cover story—the real one. I have to know."

"Things are moving, Jim. We may be able to defuse this war without any major concessions. But if, as you say, one nose is already in the tent, two is going to be just one too many."

"Have you heard from Starfleet about her status?"

"No. But the Romulans are already arguing about their own position, and the two major forces in the negotiations are sitting on information from the Hearthworlds that's making them lean toward changing their minds."

"I take it that this information has come from the inside . . ."

"You know our source," Danilov said. "Or McCoy does. An uprising is getting started on another of their colony worlds: a major one, Artaleirh. The asteroid belt around the primary there is the main source for high-quality dilithium crystals in the Imperium, and the planet itself has a great deal of heavy and high-tech industry. The Romulans could lose the system and not be crippled if it came to that, but its position is strategically critical for them. Artaleirh is far enough away from the center of things that they're concerned that the Klingons might make a move on the system from one or another of several former Rihannsu worlds they've recently occupied. But it's also close enough to ch'Rihan and ch'Havran that a failure to respond to the threat would be read as a sign of weakness by both their own people and the Klingons."

He pushed back a little in his chair, stretching, frowning. "Jim, this is distracting their attention powerfully at the moment. This whole expedition after Ael and the Sword has always been a fishing expedition for them, a way to justify what they've been planning to do anyway. But now dealing with Artaleirh is much more imperative. They're already at each other's throats about it. If we just sit right where we are, Fox says, and keep staring, and don't blink, they'll blink first and use Artaleirh as an excuse to pull back from the brink. But it's imperative that nothing else distract them right now—and most definitely not Ael. Even she'll have to admit that."

I wonder, Jim thought. "She has her own oaths, to her crew," he said, "which, to her, sometimes transcend even the disciplines of her own service. I've been in a situation like that myself, and was fortunate enough to have Fleet come down on my side, eventually." He did not add that it had taken no less a being than T'Pau of Vulcan to get them to do so. "But I would have done what I did regardless, and Ael is capable of the same level of resolve. I can give her advice, but I can't guarantee the results."

"I'm not asking you to. But Jim, please do this for me."

He stood there for a moment more, thinking about it. "All right," Jim said.

"Thank you, Jim."

Enterprise's captain fixed the commodore-in-command with a cool look. "You don't need to thank me," Jim said. "My oaths are in place. This is a duty matter. If you want to take it as a favor for a friend, that's your prerogative. But I may ask for that favor back sometime soon, and I just hope your duty won't get in the way."

Danilov simply looked at him. "We'll have to see," he said, "won't we?"

Jim nodded and went out.

"They're coming," said the scan technician, whose name Courhig could never remember.

Courhig tr'Meihan began to shake, and just stood still for a few moments until he could control that. Finally he felt himself steady down, his breathing begin to sort itself out. The image was indeed clear enough in the display—six Grand Fleet light cruisers, in formation, cruising slowly into the system.

Courhig glanced around him at the people looking
over his shoulders at the jury-rigged display and coordination panel, the hundred other people crammed
together there in the big, bare, empty hangar—men
and women, young and old, bulky enough already in
their pressure suits. It was for all the world as if
there was no room for them to spread out. But they
were hungry for closeness, all of them, at the moment. None of them had any idea how much longer
they were likely to live.

"All right," Courhig said to them. "You all know
what you have to do?"

Nods, murmurs of agreement. "Wait till we give
you the signal," Courhig said. "Don't hurry the moment until we're certain the handlers have consoli-
dated their control. If any of you have signal
failures, abort immediately and get out of the way so
that we can try to destroy whichever ship isn't responding to what we do. We can't afford to take the
chance of one of these vessels escaping with news of
what's happened."

Everyone nodded. They had heard it all a hundred
times before, in simulations and in trials, but they
knew he had to say it again.

"Then go," Courhig said. "And Elements with you
all."

"You also," some of them murmured. Then all the
pilots and crews turned and headed out the pressure
door, into the big airlock where their helms were
racked.

That door sealed behind them, and to Courhig's

ears the hiss of it was like someone's last breath. "I wish I could go with them," he said.

Behind him, Felaen stood with her arms folded, watching the displays. "We've had this discussion," she said. "You started this, and so we need you to talk to the government later—assuming that any of us survive the next thirty hours. Now just sit quiet and bear it."

He nodded. Felaen was his second-in-command mostly because she was the only one who could speak unpalatable truths to him and not be affected, or even particularly impressed, by attempts to pull rank on her afterward. There was, at the end of the day, no effective way to pull rank on one's wife.

"Gio—" he said to the tech.

"Gielo," said the tech, and laughed. It was about the tenth time it had happened.

"Gielo, sorry."

"Here's the ecliptic view, sir." The man touched several controls, and the main display, at the center of the cluster of nine, showed the outside view—the glitter of the asteroid belt seen from inside, a wide spatter of light fining down to a hard sharp glitter of it arcing away through space, toward the sun. The sensor was attached to a tower on top of the hollowed-out asteroid in which the hangar and the ships now departing were sheltered, one of hundreds that had been adapted over the past couple of centuries for storage and temporary docking. As Courhig watched, starlight shimmered above the asteroid's horizon, but he could see nothing else, and had been lucky to see that. The cloaked smallships were away, carrying with them the weapons that, if the simulations had not misled them, would start the process of making Artaleirh truly free.

Courhig found it entirely appropriate, as he stood there clenching his fists from tension and watching the display, that the technology on which those weapons were based was a spin-off from the automated rock-handling setup that had been originally invented on Artaleirh for use in this asteroid belt. Since the "handlers" had become affordable, relatively few miners bothered to actually go out in ships and wrestle with rocks anymore, now that they could sit in a comfortable room on a planet or inside an asteroid and do the wrestling from there with mechanical arms and eyes. Cheap subspace radio relaying solved the time-delay problem for those who had preferred to continue work after relocating to Artaleirh, though there were some few who still liked to stay out in the belt. For those, old habits and lifestyles died hard. Some of those old hands were the ones who were sitting at consoles elsewhere inside this rock, using virtual-reality controls to manage the handlers—the little machines that, themselves hidden with the new multiphasic cloaking device, were now making their way on detection-baffled impulse toward vessels that thought themselves invisible and, therefore, invulnerable.

Courhig watched the display that showed the tactical and tracking information. There, about five million *stai* from the asteroid belt, came the cruisers, still coasting in in formation, maintaining radio silence, looking Artaleirh over carefully from a safe distance. And meanwhile, on the other scan screens, six different readouts showed six different handlers closing in on the shimmers in space that hid the six Grand Fleet light cruisers as they braked down. One after another, as the minutes crept by, each shimmer, in its own display, suddenly gave way to views of field-attenuated, shimmery sunlight on starship hulls: the handler vehicles, precisely matching velocities with their targets, dropping slowly and gently through their cloaking fields, unseen themselves, moving closer to the vessels' hulls.

Easy, Courhig thought, *easy!* It would be too awful, after all this money spent, all this planning, all this time, to have their tactics betrayed by mere sound. But the men and women controlling the handlers were expert at maneuvering on impulse, and with the most exquisite softness, the first handler touched down on its target ship's hull and clamped tightly onto it.

Courhig and Felaen went tense, waiting for alarms, some sign of trouble. But there was none. These ships were cloaked; they thought themselves invisible, and therefore were blind to what was about to happen to them.

"They're scanning now," said the tech.

Courhig bit his lip, held himself still. This would be the last test.

"No result apparent," said the tech. "No change in course. They haven't noticed anything."

"All right," Courhig said, as one after another of the cloaked drones sat down on its target, and finally they were all in place. "Are the crews all ready?"

"All ready, *llha.*"

"Then tell the virtual warriors to turn the handlers loose." *And Earth and Fire both be with the little metal creatures.*

Courhig turned his attention to the first of the handlers to come down on one of the cruisers. He could see nothing of what it was doing: its hemispherical shape was blocking his view. But underneath it he knew that the dissolution charge was being released. That would unravel the crystalline structure of a section of the ship's hull about a cubit in diameter. A fraction of a second after that, before the hull pressure changed at all significantly, the sealing "bell" would come down over the new aperture, snugging down tight and preventing any further change in pressure. And out of the sealing bell, the "smart" cabling would come worming its way down into the 'tween-hulls space, sniffing out what it was programmed to seek: the ship's energy and communications system.

Courhig clenched his hands hard, trying not to panic. This had always been the most uncertain part of the operation in their simulations. Yet in some ways it was the simplest, for the people who had designed it were, some of them, people who had built ships for Grand Fleet in their time—and they had chosen for exploitation one of the simplest and most sensible parts of starship design. In the years since the development of silicate-based conduction conduits, Rihannsu power networks for starships had been built with what was called multiple redundancy; any cabling could carry any signal, electrical or optical. As a result, the ship's cabling network now functioned like the pathways in the brain. If one path was disabled or destroyed, a message, command, or impulse could route around the "dead" spot and get where it was going some other way. The same system carried computer linkages, comms, anything vital.

Now, though, that strength was about to be turned into a deadly weakness.

Courhig watched as the blank subscreen for that particular handler stayed blank. It was blank for a long time. *What's keeping it? Is the routine failing? Have they changed frequencies, or systems, or—* But the screen lit, then, a sudden blast of code scrolling down it, garbage characters that confirmed that the handler cable had tapped into one of the ship's networking trunks and only needed to get into synch.

Other subscreens in other displays began to show similar screenfuls of code. Courhig gulped, daring to think that it was actually going to work. The starships' computers had been programmed to protect themselves, logically enough, from commands that came from outside, from other systems. But they could not defend against ones that seemed to come from inside the ship, using the vessel's own circuitry and networking systems, seeming to belong to one of the ship's own computer terminals.

The ship did not keep secrets from itself—or not for long.

Courhig watched the first handler's programming go looking for the first piece of information it had been instructed to find and disable. Self-destruct—

"Encoded," Felaen whispered, as a string of garbage characters appeared. Courhig nodded

Then the code flashed into a string of intelligible letters and numbers. Courhig breathed out. Encrypted the information might have been, but the computer also had to store the information on how to decrypt it. Otherwise it would be useless. "Let me talk to the virtual pilots," Courhig said.

"You're on."

"Is everything going all right?" Courhig said.

The voice of Kerih, one of the oldest of them and the chief "brain" behind the handlers' programming, came back over comms. "So far," he said, "we're into three of the systems. Four. Five and six should follow shortly."

"Don't wait for them," Courhig said. "Lock down the self-destruct systems right away."

"Doing that, *llha.*"

"Then lock their helms and weapons systems," Courhig said. "Comms too. I don't want any warnings getting out."

There was a pause. Courhig stared nervously at the subscreens showing the handlers' output. All but one of them was showing results; that one was still dark.

"Done," the report came back after a moment. "All but six."

Diane Duane

"What's the matter with that one?"

"Don't know yet, *llha*," said Kerih. "Got visual from three of the other five, though."

"Good. Let me see it, and trigger the first five's invader control systems," he said. "Knock out their crews."

And now all he and Felaen could do was wait, watching repetition after repetition of the same scene: narrow views of Rihannsu officers hammering on unresponsive consoles, staggering down the corridors of their ships, trying to defend themselves and their shipmates against something they couldn't understand, then falling to the decks, overcome. Courhig should have felt triumphant, especially when the sixth subscreen finally came to life and started spilling text down itself. But instead he felt faintly sick. At least the crews had not needed killing, but these people had honestly—he assumed—been trying to do what they thought was their duty. When they were sent home after everything was finally settled—assuming that the Artaleirhin as a people, and Artaleirh itself, would survive long enough to send them back—all too likely the loyalty of the light cruisers' crews would be questioned, and a lot of them might be court-martialed and shot. Killing them cleanly might have been kinder. But that would have meant destroying the ships, and that Courhig would not do. Except . . . there was still that sixth subscreen, still dark. "Kerih, *what about six?*"

"That's *Calaf*," Kerih said, sounding unnerved. "I

just took down self-destruct and comms. Just in time too, though I don't think they got any messages out. But there's another problem—they rerouted invader control away from us somehow."

"Taif," Courrig said bitterly. He had been afraid of this. "Leave the ships locked on course out of the system for the moment," he said. "We'll have to clean them out later. Retask the smallship crews to *Calaf.* Tell them to board and neutralize the crew."

"Got that."

Courhig steadied himself on the back of Gielo's chair and swallowed hard. *Neutralize. What a nice word for it.* "I wish I were there," he said.

Felaen said nothing, just put her hands on his shoulders from behind and watched him. The five screens that were showing them images showed no new ones: only collapsed people, sleeping in smoky corridors, as they would do for hours. The ships would be followed out of system by other smallships, stopped, boarded, and their crews removed. New crews would shortly be put aboard. That in itself was a mighty success. But meantime there was still that last screen, just a stream of text . . .

It went dark.

There was a long silence.

"Kerih?" Courhig said, his voice cracking. "What happened?"

A pause. "The first two smallships made contact with *Calaf* and started forcing her hull," he said. "But somebody inside managed to override the

weapons lockdown and detonated the whole complement of photon torpedoes."

"Oh, Elements . . ." Courhig covered his face with
his hands. "Which smallships?"

"Pirrip and *Fardraw,"* Kerih said. "Some damage
to the others. Pressure leaks . . . nothing major."

Rhean, and Merik and Tuhellen, and Emmiad
with her laughing eyes, and Wraet and Sulleen . . .
Courhig wiped his eyes. *They knew the risks,
though. They were eager. There was no way I could
have stopped them.*

Too late now.

"Do you know what went wrong with that last
handler?" Courhig said finally.

"Some indications. Be hard to know for sure,
now." Kerih sounded bitter. "But next time we won't
start operations until all the handlers are live and answering properly."

"If there is a next time," Courhig said. "Grand
Fleet's not as stupid as the government, alas. They'll
work out a defense against this approach as soon as
they understand what happened. Meanwhile, we
have a little while to exploit it—maybe as long as a
month. Till then, we have other business." He turned
to Felaen. "Are the message teams ready?"

She had been bending over another console, and
now straightened up. "Already starting work," she
said. "They'll be using the handlers to pull these five
ships' last three days' communications and using
them to fabricate reports of what they're 'doing' now
that they're in system. With luck we can keep the de-

ception going for a few days—enough for us to con-
solidate our position. Enough time for other things
to happen."

He nodded. "Well," Courhig said, "let's pray that
they do. Pray to all Elements that she gets here in a
hurry. And that other help arrives hard on her heels . . .
for if it doesn't, we've got no other hope."

After seeing Danilov, Jim spent the next couple of
hours in his quarters, looking again at the slowly rotating map on the viewscreen at his desk. The computer had rendered the map in 3-D and had added
some of the star names and statuses that had come
from Ael's information. The dry Federation/new-
Bayer names and catalog numbers of the stars within
the boundaries of the Neutral Zone were now augmented by Rihannsu proper names. Apparently their
astronomers did not go in much for cataloging by
numbers, a cultural habit based in respect for the Elements and for stars and planets as "personifica-
tions" of Fire and Earth. Jim's attention was very
much on what he had defined earlier as the "second
breakout" area, the part of Romulan space closest to
both the Klingons and the Federation, and the stars
there: Orith, Mendaissa, Uriend, Artaleirh, Sam-
nethe, Ysail. Many of them had been tagged with
colors meant to show that they were being fortified,
that substantial ship squadrons had been moved
there in recent days or weeks.

"Computer," he said.

"Working."

153

"Add data on most recent Federation/Starfleet ship and troop dispositions."

Various small stars of colored light added themselves to the ones already present in the viewer. Jim had to squint a little at the display. Most of the additions were closer to the area where the talks were now being held than to the space around 15 Tri. Jim swallowed.

Even if Fox and the Intel people put this most recent info from Ael together with theirs, he thought, *it's almost too late. And if the Romulans have our information, it is too late. They'll see that Starfleet has placed its ships too far away from the "second breakout" area to stop them when they move, or to keep them from moving in the first place.*

Only a miracle can keep this war from happening now.

Jim got up, breathed out, and stood behind the desk, looking at nothing in particular. *And secretly,* he thought, *I've been expecting a miracle, just like everyone else.*

Jim stepped around the desk and went to the shelf where he kept his very few real books. Sam Cogley had taught him this particular liking, one he had been selectively indulging ever since they met, and now he reached for the book Sam had given him when they parted company after the court-martial. *Strange choice,* Jim had thought at the time, as he took the old volume down and riffled through the pages. But as he had read it he'd come to the conclusion that Sam had chosen wisely. Any starship captain was, after all, a kind of descendant of the people in these pages, journeying through a landscape as strange and unpredictable as theirs, and usually doing it with just as little backup. Now the pages fell open at the spot Jim had thought of more than once today: the story of another negotiation between distrustful parties, a long time ago.

> . . . and Arthur warned all his host that an they see any sword drawn, "Look ye come on fiercely, for I in no wise trust Sir Mordred." In like wise Sir Mordred warned his host. And so they met, and wine was fetched, and they drank. Right soon a little adder came out and stung a knight on the foot. And when the knight saw the adder, he drew his sword to kill it. When the host on both parties saw that sword drawn, then they blew trumpets and horns, and shouted grimly. Thus they fought all the day, and never stinted until many a noble knight was laid to the cold earth. . . .

Jim let out the long breath that he had been holding, thinking of the tension in that meeting room this morning, the sense of people wanting a fight and intent on getting on with it, though not without first allowing this little local drama to play itself out, so that everyone would be able to say, *We did everything we could, of course no one wants war, but you see how it is, we had no choice!* There had been the same sense of awful inevitability about the First

World War and the Eugenics Wars on Earth, and most of the great battles that had followed, right down to the last big one with the Klingons. *A shame peace isn't as inevitable,* Jim thought.

But it can be. It has *to be.*

Someone just has to set out to make it that way.

He went back to the desk, the book still in his hand, and sat looking for a long time at the image slowly rotating on the viewer's screen.

"Computer," he said at last, into the heavy, waiting silence.

"Working."

"New message. When complete, lock under voiceprint access, encrypt, and send."

"Ready."

"Begin message. Emphasize. Hold your position. Do not proceed until you hear from me. Close emphasis. The short delay may prove vital for all of us. End message. Send immediately according to routine AR-2."

"Working. Routed to Communications . . . Message sent."

Jim sat back and let out a long breath.

Now the only question is, What will she do?

Chapter Nine

WHEN THE door chimed one more time, that evening, Arrhae looked up in resignation. Earlier this evening, after the meeting of the whole negotiating group, had come yet another visit from tr'AAnikh—in a much more subdued mood than the last time, and proffering an apology. She noticed that he would not come too close to her: that, at least, made Arrhae smile. But all that while she had been nervous, for she still had not managed to identify where the bugging devices in her suite might be. She had sent tr'AAnikh away, her excuse being that she refused to accept his apology as yet—though this had left her in a foul mood, for she disliked having to act so disagreeable.

Now she got up with a frown and went to the door. Intelligence, no doubt, in the form of the miserable t'Radaik, with another of her obscure errands. She paused by the door, breathed out. "Who comes?" she said.

"A friend," said a big, deep voice.

Her eyes widened. She knew that voice, but there was no reason in space or beyond it for its owner to be outside *her* door. Nonetheless, she waved the door open.

He stood there, a little shadowy in the hallway's late-evening-scheme lighting, but unmistakable: Gurrhim tr'Siedhri. He sketched her a brief bow, one which he did not have to give her at all, and said, "Perhaps the senator might have time to speak to me."

She stood aside, and he slipped in; the door shut behind him. Arrhae waved it locked. He stood by the couch, and she blinked to see that he was actually waiting for her to sit first.

She did so, and for confusion's sake retreated into *hru'hfe* mode, saying, "May I give you something to drink, Praetor? I have here some excellent ale—"

"I take that kindly, but there is no need, and little time." He reached under his tabard.

Arrhae froze. What he brought out, though, was no weapon. It was a small sphere of dark-green metal, with several recessed touch-patches set into it, matte finish against the sheen of the rest of it. He set it down on the low table in front of the couch, and it balanced on one of the recessed patches and began to make a very small, demure humming sound. One of the patches on the side glowed a soft blue.

"It is a personal cloak," he said. "It has been set to blank out my life-sign readings; it is now also jamming whatever listening and scanning devices may have been operating in this area."

Arrhae looked at it with astonishment. Like everyone else, she had heard of such things, but had never thought to see one. Such devices were of fabulously advanced technology and expensive beyond belief, the sort of thing that only the government could afford for its own agents—it having been careful to make such technology illegal except when purchased by a government agency.

Tr'Siedhri caught Arrhae's look and gave her a dry one back. "If there is not the occasional advantage to being offensively rich," Gurrhim said, "it would be a sad thing. With this in operation, no one will know I am here. Whatever intelligence operatives are eavesdropping on you at this moment, if any, will neither see nor hear anything that occurs in here for what I intend to restrict to a very short period. They will almost certainly attribute the brief failure of their equipment to a malfunction, for this whole ship has been riddled with such; so that it would be ready for this mission, its final stages of construction were hurried through much too quickly." He smiled. "And I count it unlikely that anyone will come down here to visit. That would make it too plain that you, like everyone else aboard, were being watched, and the intel folk do so like to believe that no one knows what they are doing."

"I hope you are right," Arrhae said. "Meanwhile, the praetor's confidence honors me. Perhaps he will extend it a little—to the reason for his visit."

"Madam, you needn't be so formal with *me*," said

Gurrhim. "I am a farmer, and you are . . . an intelligent young woman whom events have raised to her proper level."

"Flatterer," Arrhae said.

He grinned, and his amiably ugly face went a little feral. "Truth sometimes wears a skewed look," he said, "while being no less true. To business, young senator. Artaleirh is in rebellion. They have declared their independence, and have also declared for the traitress."

Arrhae held very still, watching his eyes. *"Artaleirh?"* she said, taking care to sound surprised, for it was no surprise to her; the chip that tr'AAnikh had passed to Arrhae had mentioned there was trouble there. But it had not been explicit about what kind, nor had it mentioned that the planet's leadership was rising in support of Ael. That a first-generation colony world barely thirty light-years from Eisn was rebelling in so spectacular a fashion would be a blow to the Imperium indeed. "And how does this strike you?"

"As predictable," he said, "but what strikes me more is the reaction of others to the same news."

He means tr'Anierh; he would hardly be discussing the matter with me otherwise. For a moment Arrhae was irrationally distracted by a soft ticking from the heating vessel that kept water hot for herbdraft on her sideboard. But she came back to herself hurriedly. Carefully Arrhae said, "My political patron receives my reports without comment. He does not share his ideas on their content with me."

"No, that would hardly be his style," Gurrhim said. "He may use others as his sounding boards, but what song the ryill will produce after those first few testing notes, that information tr'Anierh keeps very much to himself. Such was his style in sending you here as observer. Doubtless you will have been reporting to him the reactions of others to the events now unfolding—doubtless mine as well."

It was hard to know what to do about such unadorned bluntness, a great rarity in Rihannsu of such rank. "That would seem to be a reasonable expectation on your part," Arrhae said, still watching him carefully.

Gurrhim laughed at her, though it was not an unkindly laugh. "Well," he said, "the private meeting of the senior negotiators after our whole-group meeting today was unusually lively because of this news. Hloal thought she was the only one who had heard, and thought to wrest control of the meeting to herself with it. But so many of us have come here carrying the wherewithal, in software or hardware, to carry on our business privately . . ." His smile grew ironic. "I am sure *Gorget*'s poor crew would not know where to begin if told to track down every illicit sending or receiving device aboard, or to start trying to decode all the different kinds of encrypted messages presently flowing in and out of here."

" 'Us,' " Arrhae said, concentrating on staying calm. "So you, too, have received word from outside . . ."

"Ie," he said, "and found myself in an interesting position. For the Artaleirhin have asked me to take their part and to approach the traitress on their behalf, making her aware of the support which they offer her."

"But how would you . . ." Arrhae trailed off. She could feel herself going cold, and probably pale as well. *He knows who I am. He* knows . . .

"Additionally," Gurrhim said, the smile going colder now, "Hloal and her faction have found out about the Artaleirhin's message to me. It is the excuse they have been waiting for. They will certainly kill me tonight, or try to, and dead or alive, I will be charged with treason."

The sweat broke out all over her, no stopping it. "Praetor," she said, "if this is so, then even if that does what you say it will"—she glanced at the sphere—"you may have doomed us both by coming here."

"I think not," Gurrhim said. "I think you are safe. Though Hloal and her cronies hope to upset the balance enough to oust at least one of the Three, they cannot possibly hope to do so with all of them . . . and tr'Anierh is the moderate, the balancing figure between the other two, the one most likely to survive the turmoil now beginning. An attack on you would be an attack on him. But my own fate is certainly in the balance, and who can say how it will rise or fall? So this information now passes to you, to put into your master's hand as a weapon, or to let fall unused. But consider carefully the circumstances, in either case. More—"

He bent close, as if they could even now be overheard. "Hloal and the others of her party are sure that *Bloodwing*'s commander is either already on her way back or preparing to set out. I do not know where they get this information, but they are very sure, and indeed they have so laid their nets that it seems she *must* come back. They think they have played her skillfully. We shall see. But sooner or later she must return, and some of them are intent on striking at her immediately, by surprise, meaning to take her or kill her as soon as she comes. The arguments are going on right now, and though I cannot say how long they will take, I can see already which side is likely to win, for word will shortly come from ch'Rihan to put an end to the arguing. The commanders of our ships will be instructed to take *Bloodwing*'s commander and the Sword if they can; if they cannot, they will simply destroy her and her ship, no matter how the Federation ships or Lalairu try to prevent it. And some other stroke is planned as well, something terrible, something meant to pass unnoticed in the stour that will break out when they attack her. She must be warned, Arrhae; *they* must be warned. For there is no honor in destroying an unprepared enemy."

She swallowed once, hard, at the sound of her name. Rihannsu were chary about the use of ownnames outside of family. When one appeared in conversation, it was best to listen, for one way or another, blood would likely be involved.

"Why do you come to *me* with this information?" Arrhae said.

Gurrhim gave her a sidelong look. "Has not all the world and its wife already seen you talking to MakKhoi, by the very orders of the intelligence folk here?" he said. "Why will anyone think, should you

Diane Duane

find a moment to speak to him again, or send him a message, that it is not again at their orders?"

"*One* of them will know it is not," Arrhae said. "T'Radaik."

"I count that as of no importance," Gurrhim said. "You will find a way to work around her. In your past life you will have found ways to do all manner of things without your master knowing. Why else, if you will forgive me for speaking of it, is a good *hru'hfe* so valued, except that in the leanest times there is somehow always food on the table, and no one ever accused of theft?"

The words "past life" had made her go hot and cold within seconds, in a rush of terror. That was passing now, but still Arrhae was not sure what he knew and didn't know, and half afraid to find out for sure. "Feeling as you feel about *Bloodwing*'s commander," Arrhae said at last, "—or as you allow others to think you feel—why have the Artaleirhin come to *you* with this information, this request?"

"Partly because there are ship-clan sympathizers among them," Gurrhim said, "and my loyalties are known. Partly because we have other connections. Much dilithium has been quietly diverted from its source in the Artaleirh system to other worlds farther out, for other purposes, with the help of trading companies on ch'Havran and elsewhere which I control. But more likely because the Artaleirhin know me to be, in my way, as they are: like a *shaill* of mixed blood, short, scrappy, and hard to ride, but more robust than the narrow-muzzled, thin-legged breeds that the purebreds have become in this latter day, creatures that have to be cosseted and fed their meat chopped up in little pieces. They know I have been doing in my lands, insofar as possible when one actually lives on one of the Hearthworlds, as *they* have been trying to do, farther away: running their lives as they wish to, with an eye to old law, local ways, commonsense justice. The Artaleirhin have become increasingly used to making their own way, and now they wish to do so as a freer people, in association with an empire, but not anymore as its subjects or slaves. They see *Bloodwing*'s lady as a way out of their troubles. They are willing to be a sword in her hand . . . for a while. At least they are willing to gamble, with their lives, that she will be useful to them."

She was tempted to smile at his old-fashioned manners. Nothing would bring him to speak Ael's name, which had been thrice written and thrice burned, and so did not exist, even though he was apparently willing to deal with her, even at one remove. "Why do you bring this news to me and not some other?" Arrhae said at last. "For all the sensibleness of your answer, I do not think it is merely a matter of MakKhoi."

"No," Gurrhim said, standing. "It is because I feel you are one of very few people here who did not come with a preordained agenda. Oh, I know you are tr'Anierh's creature, or must seem to be. But you seem to *me* to be in a position—and of a disposition—to judge rightly: one who will know what properly to do with this information to make the greatest difference. From what I hear, and what little I have seen of you, you seem like one who truly loves our worlds—our worlds as they ought to be, as they were once and can be again, and would be willing to risk something of value for them. *Mnhei'sahe*," he said, "you understand that, I think."

She nodded, uncertain why her eyes were starting to fill.

"And you do not flinch when you hear the word," Gurrhim said with satisfaction. "I take that as a good sign." He bent over to pick up the cloaking device, turned it over in his hands, pressed one of the patches on it.

Then he put it, heavy and cool, in her hands. "It has selfed to you, now, and will know your body readings and mask them," Gurrhim said. "It will extend range to cover me out to the lifts, then collapse the field when I am out of range. This patch"—he turned the sphere over—"will access the documentation. Hide it away, now, and do not use it unless you are in great need. Quiet night to you."

And he turned and left. Astonished, Arrhae watched him out the door, holding the thing close to her body.

Then she swallowed and hurried away to find a place to hide the cloaker, already composing in her mind her message to McCoy and trying to work out how in the worlds she was to get it to him.

* * *

Disruptor fire and phaser fire whined all around her, the deck shook with yet another explosion, and the air stank of burning plastic and scorched metal—and the other smell, the one she had not ever wanted to scent again: blood, Rihannsu and human, shed, mixed, burning. But there was no avoiding it, and the more she had tried to, the more the certainty of this moment had been pursuing her. *Better to get it over with.* She put her hand out behind her for one more phaser to set on overload and throw down that corridor, but no one put one into her hand. She turned to look over her shoulder at him.

He was not there. No one else was, either. No one stood behind her, no one waited to back her up in that charge around the corner and down the last corridor that lay between her and her desire. She was all alone. Her heart beat wildly. Mockingly, a voice said to her, *If I must go alone . . .* Her own voice.

Her eyes flew open. She saw only darkness.

The terminal on her desk chimed softly, and the sound of it reminded her when and where she was. Ael let out a breath, listened for a moment more to her heart hammering away in her side, and then sat up on her hard couch, pushing the silks away. For a moment she sat there with her fists clenched. Then she got up, made her way to the desk in the darkness, and touched the display.

"Ae."

"Khre'Riov," tr'Hrienteh's voice said, "I am sorry to wake you, but you insisted."

167

"I did, and I am glad you did. Who is it from?"

"One of the go-betweens."

She sighed. "Send it here, if you would. Then I will come up to the bridge. No point in my seeking more sleep this shift."

"I can give you something, if you like—"

Ael shook her head. "I would only fret my way through it. Better to save the drugs for when we truly need them."

"Very well, *khre'Riov*," The voice was the one tr'Hrienteh used when she was humoring a difficult patient, and Ael had to chuckle at the sound of it, for she had been hearing it a great deal recently.

"I am all right," she said. "I will be with you shortly."

"Out," tr'Hrienteh said.

Ael sat down behind the desk and waited for the message to display its usual multiple screenful of gibberish. "Analyze," she said to the computer, "and decrypt."

Obediently it did so. The message was unusually brief, even by the standards of the communiqués that came from this particular source.

> *Six Fleet light cruisers dispatched to Artaleirh now officially recognized as "missing." Nine Grand Fleet vessels have been recalled from patrol routes in the Zone nearest Laessind / RV Trianguli and are now proceeding to Artaleirh to investigate/intervene. Accordingly, Tyrava has departed to meet them.*
>
> *Advise immediately as to your intentions.*

She swallowed. This was it at last, the hinge moment on which everything would ride. Her heartbeat had been slowing, but now it began to speed again.

Ael held very still and looked across her quarters at the chair by the wall and the barely seen shadow that lay across its arms.

"Computer," she said, "record reply. I will come immediately. Will advise as to transit time. End message. Encrypt."

And there her voice failed her.

"Send?" the computer said.

Her mouth was dry. "Send."

The computer acknowledged the order, but she barely heard it. Ael got up and went to the 'fresher, put herself into it on its shortest cycle, and barely noticed that either. A few minutes later she was uniformed, out of her quarters, and on the way to the bridge.

Tr'Hrienteh was still there, working at the comms board. "I begin to think," Ael said as she swung down from the lift to where the master surgeon sat, "that you are starting to enjoy this job."

Tr'Hrienteh looked up at her. "I will enjoy it more profoundly still when my replacement is fully trained," she said, "but even he has to sleep occasionally. What orders, *khre'Riov?*"

"Get me *Ortisei*, if you would be so kind," Ael said, sitting down in her command chair. "We shall see if time has brought Captain Gutierrez wisdom."

A glance at tr'Hrienteh's expression told Ael what the surgeon thought of that possibility as she made the connection. A second or so later, the front viewscreen lit to show Ael the captain's center seat, and Gutierrez in it, looking weary. "Captain," Ael said, "a fair morning to you—assuming that our schedules are still running somewhat in tandem."

"Somewhat," Gutierrez said. "I've been trying to reach you for some time. Is there a comms problem?"

"I will investigate," Ael said, "for we have had our share of those." And that at least was true, if not specifically in this case. "Have you spoken to the commodore?"

"I have."

"That is well," Ael said, "for I can wait no longer; we must return to RV Trianguli."

"The commodore," Gutierrez said, "when I spoke to him six hours ago, instructed me to attempt to dissuade you from making such a move right now."

"You may try, but you will achieve no result you desire, Captain. I am sorry."

Gutierrez looked at her in silence for a moment. "That being the case," he said then, "Commodore Danilov has instructed me to accompany you wherever you go. If you would have your navs officer coordinate with mine, we can leave immediately for RV Tri, if you insist on going now, and be there within two standard hours."

"I do insist," Ael said. *But how interesting. Either Ddan'ilof has realized that he sent too few ships with* Bloodwing *to enforce any order, or someone in Starfleet or elsewhere has become willing to allow this matter to come to a swifter conclusion. I sup-*

pose I should be grateful that for once we agree . . . but it is unusual . . .

She glanced at Khiy. "Arrange matters with *Ortisei*'s helm officer immediately," she said. "And meanwhile, Captain, I thank you for your assistance. Is there anything else needs saying before we go?"

He gave her what for a human was a fairly dry look. "Don't do anything cute."

"Why, Captain, if I understand your idiom correctly, you have nothing to fear. Returning to RV Trianguli is all my desire." *For the moment . . . until what waits there has been dealt with. And after that, we will not linger.*

"I'm delighted to be able to oblige you," Gutierrez said. He glanced at his helm officer. "Feeding you coordinates now, Commander. If you would pace us at warp seven?"

"So ordered. I thank you, Captain." She gave him about a fingerjoint's-depth of bow and then glanced sideways at tr'Hrienteh, who killed the connection.

"And now for it," Ael said, straightening, as the warp drive came on line and Khiy took *Bloodwing* out along the course indicated. "All crew to alert stations. Run the priming checks on the weapons systems but do not bring them up to 'hot' status, not yet. Shields up, and have the cloak ready, but do not under any circumstances implement it until I give the word."

She glanced around her cramped little bridge and saw everyone bending to their instruments with the familiar looks of concentration, and a little more besides: excitement. It was beginning to stir in her, as well. "Aidoann," she said, "I have a few things to set in order. I will be in my quarters for a short time, and then down in engineering, if you need me."

"Yes, *khre'Riov,*" Aidoann said and smiled with that feral little look of eager preparedness that Ael had come to depend on over time. It was very unlike Tafv's old calm, which had always set in harder the more excited he got.

She sighed. *Very unlike.* And she thought, as she got into the lift, *How strange. This is the first time I have thought of him today. Not so long ago he would have been my first thought after waking.*

He is finally beginning to slip away from me.

But is this a bad thing?

In her quarters, Ael moved around, putting away those few things she had taken out of their storage cupboards over the past couple of days' quiet time— the clumsy cast-ceramic bird figurine Tafv had made as a present for her when he was little, the old hardcopy notebook from her days in the Colleges of the Great Art—and folded away the couch. Then she slipped around to sit at the desk again, and found the terminal's screen blinking with the notifier herald that indicated another message waiting for her. Apparently it had been waiting long enough that the audio signal had turned itself off.

"Analyze," she said, "and decrypt."

The characters on the screen descrambled themselves, leaving her looking at another very short message. It was from Jim.

For once the name did not bring the customary smile to her lips as she read the message. Ael leaned on her elbows, laced her fingers together, leaned her chin on them, and looked at the screen.

It is not too late to change my mind. Though doubtless it would irk poor Gutierrez, despite the fact that we would be following Ddan'ilof's wishes.

Yet here she could see the commodore's hand at work, and she did not trust his motives. She trusted Jim's, but at the same time the captain was subordinate to Ddan'ilof, and had little choice about obeying his orders. Though if the captain agreed with the commodore's reasons . . .

After a moment Ael unlaced her fingers and reached out to touch the comms control on the display. But then she stopped herself.

They do not know what I know about Artaleirh . . . or about Tyrava. *And I have already told those who are waiting for us that I am on my way.*

I cannot do as he asks. And just now, I dare not tell him why. It must wait.

"No reply. Store," she said.

"Stored."

Ael stared at the blanked screen for a moment more, and then got up and went out, making for the engine room and one last consultation with tr'Keirianh.

In the dim late-night lighting of the corridor aboard *Gorget*, Arrhae pressed the door signal one more time. She was starting to get impatient, and letting it show for the benefit of any scanner. She was just lifting a fist to bang on the door when it slid open.

Tr'AAnikh stood there in rather charming disarray, barefoot, breeches pulled on hastily, and one of his sleeping silks draped around his torso for modesty's sake. His eyes widened at the sight of Arrhae. She swept straight past him into his cubbyhole, taking it all in at a glance—in fact, it was hard not to, it was so small: couch-pallet, silks, clothes cupboard, a very minimal 'fresher. As the door shut she turned to face him again, wearing an expression of careful disdain. "I have decided," Arrhae said, "how I may after all allow you to do me a service as penance for your recent crude behavior."

"You have? I mean, ah, yes, you have," tr'AAnikh said, running a hand through his hair as if trying to push it into some kind of order, and failing.

"Yes. Now straighten up and attend me, tr'AAnikh. You have been running documents back and forth several times each day from your mistress's office to Ambassador Fox's, I understand."

"Yes, noble *deihu*," he said, looking more bemused every moment.

"Very well. It will be morning in a matter of an hour or so aboard their ships. I require you to deliver this package to the ambassador's office for me, along with whatever else you would normally be taking there on your first errand."

She thrust the film-wrapped box she had been carrying at him, and tr'AAnikh took it and stared at it. "What is it, noble lady?"

"As if that's any of your business," Arrhae said. "Or as if I need to explain myself to such as you. It's a flask of ale. I was rather abrupt with the poor doctor the other evening—more so than necessary, in the face of what he intended as a courtesy. And good behavior should be reinforced, even when it's aliens and barbarians evincing it. He has a taste for ale, apparently, and I've enough of the stuff in my suite to swim in if I chose. I can easily enough spare him a bottle. So see to it that this comes to him without delay. The ambassador's assistant will manage it."

"Uh," tr'AAnikh said.

"Without delay," Arrhae said, her eyes locking with his, "or you'll smart for it. Your mistress asked me how I wanted you punished for your behavior. I've given her no answer yet. If you prove dilatory in this, I'll think of something with great speed. Now be about it."

And very, very slightly, as he bowed to her, she winked at him.

The bow got caught for just a fraction of a second, then went deep. "Noble *deihu,* I will attend to it instantly," tr'AAnikh said.

Arrhae sniffed and swept out of the tiny cabin, hearing behind her, as the door closed, the sound of someone starting very hurriedly to get dressed.

Now, she thought as she made her way casually back to her suite, *the matter is in the Elements' domain. Let Them speed the message to where it needs to be . . .*

She had barely made it inside and shut the door

before a dreadful noise erupted in her suite, and as far as she could tell, everywhere in the ship. Her first horrified thought was that she was already betrayed, that someone had scanned that bottle preparatory to beaming it out. Ffairrl came immediately out of his little galley-room, where he had been preparing breakfast.

"What in the worlds *is* that?" Arrhae said, not having to work very hard to sound frightened.

"Security alert," Ffairrl said. "The level just below battle stations." He looked pale.

And then the terminal on the desk in her office started chiming urgently for attention.

Arrhae swallowed once, then went in and touched it awake. "I-Khellian," she said.

"Deihu—" The face looking at her from the screen was one she did not know, a young man with light hair, but the uniform was Intelligence green-sashed black. "Are you all right? Is everything well there?"

"Yes, everything is fine, except for that dreadful noise," Arrhae said. "What's amiss?"

"Someone has shot the praetor Gurrhim tr'Sied-hri," the young officer said. "We are checking on everyone in the delegation while the ship is searched for the perpetrator and the weapon. Please stay in your quarters until the search is complete, *deihu,* and assist the search party when they arrive."

"Of course. But the praetor, is he . . ."

"Living still. He is in the infirmary. But his injuries are severe, and the surgeons are uncertain whether they can save him . . ."

"Thank you," Arrhae said, and touched the connection off.

She looked up and saw Ffairrl looking in the office door at her. Her mind was in turmoil. "You heard that?" she said.

"I could not help it, noble *deihu.*"

"Terrible," she said. "Terrible . . ." She walked out into the main room again, while one thought burned hot in her brain: *Whoever tried to kill him will find it all too easy to finish the job in the infirmary—assuming the surgeons themselves are not even now being told to do so, by action or inaction. Either way, he will not survive if he remains aboard* Gorget.

She poured herself a cup of herbdraft from the sideboard. "My appetite will be worth nothing until this searching is over," she said. "This will suffice me for now. Meanwhile, Ffairrl, will you do something for me?"

"Certainly, noble *deihu.*"

"I am minded to accept young tr'AAnikh's apology now," she said. "He has shown himself contrite enough that I can afford to be gracious about his lapse. You know where his quarters are?"

"I can find them, *deihu.*"

"Go do so, then, and tell him he may wait on me without delay as soon as he has completed the other errand I gave him. Say just that to him."

Ffairrl bowed. "I will deliver your message exactly so, *deihu.*" He made for the door.

"Oh, and Ffairrl—" He paused. She smiled very slightly, with a conspiratorial look. "When he arrives, I will wish to be private with him for an hour or so. See to it."

"But, lady, if the searchers come while—"

"Certainly nothing is going to happen until they have left," Arrhae said, sounding scornful. "On *that* you may depend. Now go."

He went.

Arrhae glanced at the cupboard. The little cloaking sphere lay in a bottom drawer, under a pile of bodysilks. *Where can I possibly hide it so they will not find it? If they—*

The door signal went off.

She got up and went to answer it. The door slid open to reveal six people, three men and two women in the gray-on-black of ship's security, and one in Intel black and green, all bearing various kinds of scanning equipment. "Noble *deihu*," the Intel officer said, "we beg your pardon, but we—"

"Yes, yes, come in and get it over with," Arrhae said, "so that I can get back to my mornmeal before it grows cold."

They filed in and walked around the room, which soon filled with the hum and buzz of their scan equipment. Arrhae sat down and drank her draft and pointedly ignored them all, fighting not to look as nervous as she felt, while they went into Ffairrl's little galley, all over her suite and into her bathroom, scanning every piece of furniture in the place, and every drawer and cupboard. But the moment she was dreading, the sound of one of their scanners going off as it discovered something suspicious, never came. Finally one of them opened the clothespress and started scanning in there, and when he was finished, even started opening the drawers.

Now or never. Arrhae looked over at him, the last one left looking for anything; the rest were gathered together in the middle of the room, comparing readings, plainly having had only negative results. In a voice dripping with lazy scorn, Arrhae said, "If with all your high-priced machinery you have found nothing, I think you may safely leave off pawing through a senator's intimates, fellow. Unless you and your comrades prefer to find yourselves pawing through something far less attractive, on your account, when we get back home . . ."

The security man, who had been about to open that last drawer, started straight up as if shocked. "Close that up straightway," the Intelligence officer said, irritated, "and come along. *Deihu,* a thousand pardons for troubling your morning."

And out they went.

Arrhae sat right where she was for a few seconds, trying to find her composure again. *It not only kept poor Gurrhim from being detected,* she thought, *but it has protected itself from detection as well.*

The small relief did nothing to assuage her greater concern. *Well. If this does not qualify as a great need . . .* For something in her was saying, *Keep that man alive. Whatever you do, keep him alive!*

Arrhae got up, waved the door locked, and went to get the sphere. For the next little while she sat in the bathroom with the door closed, hurriedly speed-reading her way through the holographic projection it produced of its documentation. And by the time the door signal went again, she was ready.

She stuffed the sphere into her breeches pocket and went to answer the door. Tr'AAnikh was standing there, looking somewhat apprehensive.

"*Deihu* . . ." he said.

"Come in," Arrhae said. "And sit down. We must have a talk . . ."

The building in which the Senate kept its administrative offices was only across the Avenue of Processions from the great domed building itself, but even so close, no whisper of the noise of reconstruction came through the plasteel of the window that made up one whole wall. Everything was silent in the small, bare retiring room where the three men now stood. It looked as if it should have echoed, for there was not so much as a stick of furniture in it, and the floor and walls were bare. But every word spoken sounded almost painfully anechoic due to the damping devices in operation. No force known to Rihannsu science could see or hear what was happening in that room . . . which was the way the three men wanted it.

"We should at least get it back."

"There's no *point* in it now, Arhm'n! It's a liability. Trying to save it will only multiply the chances that she'll somehow escape alive. And we cannot permit that now. We have to kill her immediately, while we have the chance."

"I'm not saying *that's* a bad idea. You know how I feel, Urellh! But the Sword—"

"It no longer *matters*. There's far worse to deal with now. If we're concerned about keeping our people in line, well, the Klingons will be giving us more than enough fuel for that fire momentarily. Maybe it's a blessing in disguise; nothing unifies a people like a good war, eh? But whatever happens, if we are not to have Artaleirh, *they* certainly cannot be permitted to have it. The place is going to be destroyed anyway; it makes little odds which of us does it now. No news will come from there to ch'Rihan and ch'Havran that we don't permit to come . . . and after the fact, we can present that news any way we like. But there's time to worry about that later."

"My people in the Fleet will handle it. But the Sword—"

"Let it be *lost,* for Fire's sake, Arhm'n! It's *her* the damned Artaleirhin are after, not what she stole. She is poison, that woman! Kill her now before she becomes some kind of symbol for noble rebellion."

"Before the sickness spreads any further," said the third man. "And the Sword is also likely to be contaminated forever after by its association with her; it will be no more use to us as a symbol. The news of its loss can be managed, too. As that of tr'Siedhri's death, when that finally happens."

"Damn the man, is he unable to cooperate with *anything?* I thought he would have died by now—"

"Still 'critical,' " Urellh said. "Well, he can't last long in *Gorget's* infirmary; he needs surgical routines with which they're not equipped to provide him. And their master surgeon knows which way the wind is blowing; he'll do nothing heroic. Never mind farmer Gurrhim—he's paid for his treason, and he'll soon be mucking out the Elements' stables. As for t'Rllaillieu, Arhm'n, capture and trial are now the wrong way to handle her. She must die immediately, before she can do any more damage."

There was a long silence. Arhm'n looked at tr'Anierh.

"Expediency," tr'Anierh said, "I think, requires this of us now. This unrest is caused—and spread— by uncertainty. The best way to settle the unrest is by providing the rebels and would-be rebels with a certainty they cannot contest: that she is finally gone, forever, beyond any possibility of rescue, exculpation, or pardon. Let us make it unanimous, Arhm'n. In the present circumstances, we three must not be seen to be divided. Too much rests on it."

The silence stretched out.

"Tell them to go ahead with it, then," Arhm'n muttered. He stood watching them taking the scaffolding away from the great dome across the way. "Problems may be multiplying at the moment, but shortly their number will decrease by one . . . one very *large* one."

Sleep forsook Jim early that morning, after only a few hours, and would not come back. The clock was ticking toward Fox's deadline, and the tension ruined his sleep. By the time he had breakfast and got up to the bridge, it was still only seven hours until the meeting at which Ael's status would be clarified, and everything would blow up, one way or another. And there had been no answer from Ael, even though Jim knew she might send none even if she agreed with him. Her concerns about the security of information on her own ship could well be behind the silence.

On the bridge, Mr. Spock was standing at his viewer, looking down it steadily, making delicate adjustments at one side of it, and he did not look up at the sound of the lift doors opening and shutting. Jim went and sat down in the center seat, and when the morning duty yeoman came to him with the order-of-the-day padd, he said softly, "How long has he been at it, Ms. Nyarla?"

The tall, dark-haired ensign glanced over at Spock and said as softly, "At least since I first came in, Captain: three hours and fifty-four minutes ago."

Jim nodded as he looked down the padd and initialed the bottom of it. A Syan had a circadian-based clock in her head as accurate as Spock's, for different reasons, so the phrasing was nothing unusual. But her presence here was. "You're not supposed to be on for a couple of hours yet," Jim said.

She raised her eyebrows. "After I finish budding," she said, "I'm always on edge. Present circumstances . . ."

"Understood," Jim said, and handed her back the stylus and the padd. "Did that go smoothly, by the way?"

"No problems, Captain," Nyarla said. "Except, as

usual, the new personality is starting to complain about wanting her own quarters." She put up her eyebrows, looking resigned. "Same as always. 'Twelve's a crowd . . .' "

"Well, let the doctor know if it starts to be a problem."

"I will, sir." She headed for the turbolift. Jim raised his eyebrows, once again making a mental note to ask McCoy exactly how he dealt with a crewman who budded off a new subsection of her brain, and hence a new personality, every eight months or so. Though probably McCoy would refuse to tell him much, on confidentiality grounds.

Sulu came in as Nyarla went out. He relieved the duty helmsman and started checking out his console. Jim glanced over his shoulder and saw that Scotty's station was empty. "Lieutenant, has Mr. Scott come on duty yet?" he said to Uhura.

"Came in and went out again half an hour ago, Captain," she said. "He's down in engineering with K's't'lk and a couple of his staff, going over some new Sunseed numbers, he said."

Jim nodded. Everything running with the usual efficiency, but a little ahead of schedule. *Everybody else around here is getting as twitchy as I am,* he thought. *It can be a good thing . . . within reason. If the tension gets so great that it starts affecting response times . . .*

Spock straightened up, though he was still looking down at the scanner as if he distrusted what he had been seeing. Jim glanced back at him. "The Romulans still busy with their long-range scanning, Mr. Spock?"

"They are," Spock said. "But that is not my concern at the moment."

"It's not?"

Spock left the science station and came down to stand by the center seat. "The scanning I have been monitoring is of a sort I have not seen in previous encounters with Romulan vessels," he said. "It suggests they may have made some theoretical breakthroughs in their understanding of the nature and structure of subspace, and further analysis will be interesting. I have begun work on such analysis. But while monitoring the scanning activity, I also detected some interesting energy readings from two of the ships, *Pillion* and *Hheirant.*"

"Interesting? In what way?"

Spock raised his eyebrows. Jim had seen this expression before: it was that of a Vulcan who cannot admit to annoyance, but is experiencing it nonetheless. "Our own scans seem to be detecting power generation from within both *Pillion* and *Hheirant* considerably in excess of what ships of their size should require either for maximum projected propulsion or for maximum weapons use, or, for that matter, for both together. And if this were not in itself cause enough for interest, I am unable to determine from exactly what system aboard these ships the power in question is being generated, except that it does not appear to be directly associated with their engine rooms."

"Some kind of weapon we haven't been told about?" Jim said.

Spock let out a breath. "Insufficient data," he said.

"Our own scans are not proving as efficient as they should, especially considering that we are at such close range. I have recalibrated our scanners twice within the last three hours, with only marginal improvement in the resulting scans."

"And it's nothing to do with *Mascrar* being in the way?"

"No, Captain."

Jim thought for a moment. "Some variant on the cloaking device?"

"That is a theory that had occurred to me, Captain, but the typical waveform signature of the cloaking device we know is missing. That does not, of course, rule out the possibility that a new one has been developed, and there are some waveforms presenting in the scans from *Pillion* and *Hheirant* which I do not recognize, but there is as yet no evidence to support the conjecture that they are associated with new cloaking technology. They could, for example, be parasitic on the ships' communications systems. But unless I can improve the quality of our own scanning, there is no way either to confirm this or to rule it out."

Jim's attention went to the main viewscreen. He could just catch sight of one of *Gorget*'s long, swept-back nacelles below the curve of *Mascrar.* "There's a lot of new technology out there," he said. "Some of it has plainly been brought to impress us."

"But what I am picking up is not associated with the newer ships, Captain. *Pillion* and *Hheirant* are two of the older *K'tinga*-class models."

"Well, stay on it, Mr. Spock. I'll be interested to see what you find."

Spock nodded and went back up to his science station. The turbolift doors opened, and McCoy came ambling in. "I don't suppose," he said, "that anything's happened to make them have that meeting early."

"What do *you* think?" Jim said.

"Well, hope springs eternal . . ."

"Oh, Doctor," Uhura said, "while you're here—a message just came in for you from *Speedwell*, from the ambassador's office."

"For me?" McCoy said. "What the heck do they want from me?"

"It's nothing they want *from* you. They have something *for* you. A package. It came over from *Gorget*, apparently, with this morning's documents exchange."

Jim looked at McCoy, wondering. McCoy raised his eyebrows. "Did they scan it? Do they have any idea what it is?"

"The ambassador's assistant says it checks clean for explosives or other dangerous devices. He says it's a bottle."

McCoy smiled slightly. "Ale, I bet," he said. "Shows you what the explosives scan's worth. Ask them to beam it over, would you?"

"They'll be doing that shortly."

"Fine, I'll go on down and get it."

Uhura chuckled then. "My, we're busy this morning. Captain, I have Commodore Danilov waiting for you, scrambled."

"Put him on," Jim said.

The screen flickered, and there was Danilov, looking pleased. "Jim," he said, "I wanted to thank you again for that message you sent."

"No need, Commodore," Jim said, rather surprised.

"I disagree," Danilov said. "We just got in a message from one of the Zone monitoring stations. Long-range scan shows that a number of Romulan vessels that were patrolling the other side of the Neutral Zone near here have pulled out."

So Fox was right, Jim thought. *They're starting to blink.*

Or so it seems.

"There's something else you should know about," Danilov said. "Apparently things are breaking apart somewhat among the Romulan negotiation team. One of the praetors, Gurrhim tr'Siedhri, is in the infirmary aboard *Gorget,* subsequent to an assassination attempt."

"Good Lord," Jim said. "How is he?"

"No details," Danilov said. "Fox thinks this is symptomatic of a serious split among the senior negotiators. We'll see what happens at the meeting later."

"Have we heard back from Earth yet about Ael?" Jim said.

"We have," Danilov said. "Later, Jim. *Speedwell* out."

The screen flicked back to its view of *Mascrar* and the other vessels orbiting on this side with *Enterprise.* Jim sat back in the center seat and let out a breath of exasperation. *I am* not *cut out for this diplomatic work,* he thought.

Nonetheless, he settled in to wait.

Half an hour or so later, McCoy was leaning against the transporter console in Transporter Room Two, trying to control his impatience and failing. "What's *keepin'* those people?" he said.

"Something to do with the assassination attempt aboard *Gorget*," said the transporter chief. "None of the diplomatic people are where they'd usually be. The transporter chief over on *Speedwell* says she sent most of the ambassador's people over to *Mascrar.* The rest could have used another transporter."

"Typical," McCoy muttered. He reached out to the comm button, hit it. *"Speedwell,* this is McCoy aboard *Enterprise.* Can somebody please track down this package or bottle or whatever it is that the ambassador's office is holding for me? I have other things to do today . . ."

"Hold on a moment, Doctor," said a somewhat bored male voice. Then another voice, a female one, said, "Chief Perelli, shuttle bay. We've got a kind of long box here. It's annotated as 'bottle' on the docs manifest the courier brought over this morning."

"That's sounds like what we're after. Would you run it up here?"

"Sure thing. Sorry for the delay, Doctor. This is medicinal, right?"

McCoy grinned. "If you get a chance to come over here, I'll let you see *how* medicinal."

A few minutes later there was a sparkle on one of the frontmost transporter pads, and a box wrapped in silvery prismatic plastic appeared. "Thanks, Chief," McCoy said, going over to pick it up.

"Hey, don't *I* get any?"

"Come see me when you're off duty. You're due for your multipox inoculation anyway; you can have that at the same time."

"Uh . . . thanks."

McCoy chuckled as he made his way out of the transporter room and back to sickbay. Slender, curly-haired Lia Burke, who was still holding down the head nurse's position in sickbay while Christine Chapel was away presenting her doctoral dissertation, met McCoy going out as he came in, and glanced at what he was holding. "Oh, you got your bottle, finally."

"Yes. And you can't have any."

"Hmph."

"While on duty," McCoy added belatedly as the door closed behind her. He went to his desk and picked up a phaser scalpel lying there, and started to use it delicately on the end of the package. The wrapping shriveled away, revealing a prosaic box. He upended it, looking for the opening. He found the seal and ran a thumbnail along it.

The side of the box opened up. Inside there was something silky and black, with a faint touch of fragrance about it, a warmly herbal scent. McCoy looked at it with a moment's affection, but the warmth suddenly faded as he considered what this might mean.

He pulled the long, diaphanous scarf out of the

box from around the bottle for which it had been used as wrapping, and ran it quickly through his hands. There was nothing hidden in the seams this time. But it was a message nonetheless.

McCoy picked up his medical scanner from the instrument tray nearby and ran it down the length of the scarf, just to make sure. Nothing.

Then he reached into the box and pulled out the bottle. The ale in it was unusually blue, the sign of a good "vintage," at least a couple of weeks old. More, it had that slight cloudiness of *really* good Romulan ale, an indication that all the fruit solids hadn't been filtered out of it. *Also,* McCoy thought, as he ran the scanner over the bottle, *it makes it that much harder to see anything that might be inside.*

The medical scanner chirruped twice, the alert sound it made when it found embedded data content in a sample but couldn't immediately read it.

McCoy's eyes widened. He took himself and the bottle out of sickbay in a hurry, heading for the bridge.

Spock was still staring down his scanner. Jim was wondering if this wasn't beginning to get a little obsessive. Still, there had been enough times before when Spock had focused on a problem until he wore himself thin, and his persistence had wound up being the only thing that saved *Enterprise* and everyone in her—one more aspect of her charmed life, too easily overlooked when outsiders examined the legend. Jim sat back and sighed. "Uhura—" he said.

Diane Duane

"Another hour yet till the meeting, Captain." She sighed too.

He had to smile. "Spock," he said, "find anything worthwhile yet?"

Spock shook his head without looking up from the scanner. "Their long-range scans continue. Over the past twenty minutes I have seen that odd waveform again in several brief bursts, each several seconds long, from what seem to be two different sources associated with *Pillion* and *Hheirant*. But then the traces faded out entirely. I am at a loss to understand it. I begin to wonder whether I am detecting some sort of malfunction, except that—"

The turbolift doors opened. "Mr. Spock! Here! Quick!"

Jim turned around, surprised to hear McCoy so out of breath. Spock had looked up from his scanning with a rather severe expression, for McCoy was standing there next to him, holding a bottle of something blue. "Doctor," Spock said, "this is hardly the time or the place—"

"Spock," McCoy growled, "I've always thought you needed a humoroplasty, but by God as soon as I have two seconds to rub together, I'm going to change your surgery status from elective to required." He shoved the bottle at Spock. "Now in the name of everything that's holy, scan this thing and find out what it *says!*"

Nonplussed, Spock took the bottle and looked it over, then sat it on his science console and touched several controls. He put up one eyebrow. "There is a picochip attached under the stopper," Spock said, and hurriedly touched several more controls in sequence. "Reading now . . ."

The screen nearest his station filled with gibberish, which then started to resolve itself.

He stared at it, then turned toward the center seat. "It is from Lieutenant Haleakala-LoBrutto," Spock said. "She reports that the Romulans intend to attack and destroy *Bloodwing* immediately on her return to the system—"

"Warp ingress, Captain," Sulu said urgently. "Two vessels going subluminal, ten light-seconds out."

"Uhura, copy that message to *Speedwell* and the other ships right away!" Jim said. "Mr. Sulu, take us out toward the ingress point, full impulse. Put it on screen. Mr. Chekov, ready phasers and photon torpedoes."

"Enterprise," Danilov's voice said over the comm link, "where do you think you're going? Hold your position—"

"Read your mail, Dan!" Jim said. "Mr. Chekov—"

"Phasers ready, Captain. Photon torpedoes loading."

"Mr. Sulu, what are the Romulans doing?"

"Nothing, Captain. Holding position. No evidence of weapons activity."

"There is more to the lieutenant's message, Captain," Spock said. "She warns of an imminent clandestine attack of a major and devastating nature on Federation space."

"Mr. Chekov, raise shields—" But Jim's attention was distracted by an alarm indicator that suddenly began to flash at Sulu's position at the helm console.

Sulu, busy with taking *Enterprise* away from *Mascrar* and the rest of the Federation task force without immediately exposing her to the Romulans on the other side of the habitat, glanced at it and said, "Intruder alert, Captain!"

The intercom whistled. "Bridge," Scotty's voice said, "we've got someone beaming aboard from one of the other ships. The transport signature's Romulan!"

"Shields!"

"Up now, Captain."

Too late, Jim thought. "Scotty, where's the intruder beaming to?"

"Transporter Room Two."

"Seal that deck off. Get a security detail down there on the double." He gripped the arms of the center seat, resisting the urge to jump up and see what the hell was going on. "Mr. Sulu, are we secure now?"

"Yes, Captain. Heading for the ingress point. Two ships coming in, decelerating from warp, down to about point two C now."

On screen, with magnification, you could just see them, two sparks coasting inward in RV Trianguli's hot blue light. "Uhura," Jim said, "send to both ships. *Ortisei, Bloodwing,* break away, you are about to come under attack!"

"Enterprise," came another voice. It was the city manager from *Mascrar,* sounding rather alarmed. "You are not scheduled to leave formation at this time, and your movements and signals may be misconstrued—"

"Captain, I am picking up impulse engine activity out there," Chekov said, working over his console.

"But all ships in the system are in position and accounted for, none of them can be producing it!"

"The new waveform I detected earlier is associated with the impulse engine readings," Spock said suddenly. "I believe your conjecture was correct, Captain. The source of the readings is accelerating toward *Ortisei* and *Bloodwing*. But there is still a peculiarity." Spock stared down his scanner, manipulating it. "I cannot tell whether it is one impulse engine or two. It is ghosting, phasing in and out."

"Mr. Chekov, lock weapons on that impulse engine reading and prepare to fire. Try to refine the scan, though! Mr. Sulu—"

"*Enterprise,* I warn you, if you open fire, we will act to enforce the neutrality of the space around us!"

"*Mascrar,* scan ahead of us, it's not *our* fire you need to be worrying about! What about that impulse engine, attached to a ship that we can't see? Sulu, position!"

"Four light-seconds out at bearing one one five mark six, Captain. Closing on *Ortisei* and *Bloodwing.*"

"Oh, my God," McCoy said softly. "This is it."

"Security to Captain Kirk," a voice said. "Lieutenant Harmon here—"

"Report!" Jim said.

"Three Romulans have beamed aboard, Captain," said Harmon. "All male. All three are wounded, two severely. Those two are unconscious. The conscious one is asking specifically for Dr. McCoy."

"Get them straight down to sickbay," McCoy said. "I'll meet you there. Uhura, page Dr. M'Benga and have him report there immediately. Sickbay, Burke!"

"Burke here, Doctor."

"Incoming wounded. Romulan. Break out the Vulcaniform trauma packs. You're going to have a security team in there in about three minutes, and I'll be there in about five. Triage the wounded, stabilize them, and activate scrub fields as necessary." And he was gone.

Jim turned his attention back to the screen. There was nothing to be seen out in the starry darkness but *Bloodwing* and *Ortisei,* coasting in. "The other Federation vessels are going to alert status," Chekov said. "Shields going up. Romulan vessels are doing the same. Their weapons systems are heating up—"

And when the host on both parties saw that sword drawn . . . But if the sword was *not* drawn, lives were going to be lost. He knew it. *"Ortisei!"* Jim said. "Afterburner, can you see the impulse reading approaching you? Fire at it, it's going to attack!"

"Bloodwing is breaking away," Sulu said. "The vessel running on impulse is changing course to intercept."

"Both *Ortisei* and *Bloodwing* have raised shields," Chekov said. "Weapons systems aboard *Bloodwing* coming on line—"

"Enterprise, I have orders not to fire unless fired upon," Gutierrez's voice came back. "You have the same orders, Jim. I can see a faint impulse track, all right, but there's no sign of any cloaking device in use—"

"I am a fool," Spock said.

The statement was so bald and so flat that even in

these circumstances, Jim had to glance over at Spock in astonishment. "What?"

"I have misread data which has been in front of me for many hours," Spock said, his voice tight. "The name *Pillion,* Captain! It is not just a name. It could be taken for such, for the Romulans often name ships after the accoutrements of an armed warrior: *Gorget, Helm,* and so on. A pillion is a saddle. But it is also an extra pad fastened behind a regular saddle so that another rider can use the same conveyance. To ride pillion is to ride two on a mount."

Jim's eyes widened. "Oh, my God," he said, turning back to the screen.

"The impulse signature is changing," Sulu said. "Two signatures, Captain, not one. One heading toward *Ortisei* now!"

"*Pillion* has been carrying at least one second vessel, which remained cloaked even though the primary one was uncloaked and visible," Spock said. "They must have achieved a major breakthrough in the design of the cloaking device to be able to produce such an effect, especially one which would withstand visual and scan inspection at such close range. That is the vessel responsible for the attack we have just seen."

Jim swallowed. This information alone qualified as one of the triggers that would activate his sealed orders, but he had little time to spare for that issue now. *Ortisei* and *Bloodwing* were getting closer. "The impulse sources continue to accelerate," Chekov said. "One is now within conventional phaser range of *Ortisei.* Captain, shall I fire?"

He stared at the screen. It had never occurred to him that the sword to be drawn would be in *his* hand. He opened his mouth to tell Sulu to fire.

In the space between *Ortisei* and *Bloodwing,* the stars suddenly began to shimmer.

And *Bloodwing,* as she curved away, fired her phasers, nearly point-blank, right at *Ortisei.*

Between the two of them, where space had been shimmering, only one spread of torpedoes had time to come blasting out from the little half-decloaked ship before it blossomed into a tremendous explosion. *Bloodwing* twisted and arced away from the explosion and the remaining torpedoes, and on the other side, *Ortisei,* having just begun an evasive maneuver, shuddered and sideslipped as the force of the explosion hit her shields.

And everything started to happen at once. All the Romulan ships but *Gorget* left their positions on the far side of *Mascrar* and started to move with increasing speed toward *Bloodwing. Bloodwing,* recovering from her evasive maneuvers, threw herself straight at the Romulan vessels, firing.

"Captain!" Chekov said. "The torpedoes that the cloaked vessel launched—*they're coming back!*"

"Evasive," Jim said.

"They appear to be tracking *Bloodwing,*" Spock said. "Difficult to determine whether they are targeting the ship's ID, or just her engine type."

Bloodwing streaked past *Ortisei,* which was drifting now, a terrible flickering running up and down her starboard nacelle. The torpedoes followed, and the Romulan vessels, seeing her coming, scattered . . .

. . . but not fast enough. One torpedo, its tracking computers possibly confused by all the other Romulan engines in the area or deranged by the explosion of the originating vessel when it first fired, slammed into *Thraiset*, whose shields flared into a globe of fire and then collapsed. A second torpedo coming right behind the first one hit *Thraiset* amidships, and the ship instantly bloomed into a white fury of fire as its antimatter catastrophically annihilated.

"Brace for impact!" Jim yelled. Even with shields up, *Enterprise* rocked and plunged as the shock wave from the matter/antimatter annihilation hit her. The lights wavered and the artificial gravity flickered once or twice, but not severely enough to throw people around. "Damage report!"

Spock was reading his console. "Reports coming in from decks six, eight, nine forward." he said. "Some injuries, no major structural damage. Shields down to sixty percent, they will take some time to recharge—"

Jim's heart was pounding. It was a captain's worst nightmare, everything happening at once, no way and no time to limit the damage. *Ortisei* was still drifting, the discharge-flicker around her nacelle gone now. *"Ortisei* is evacuating her crew to *Mascrar,"* Uhura said. "Matter-antimatter containment is holding, but they're not taking any chances."

That at least was some consolation. "Mr. Sulu, go after those torpedoes," Jim said, "before this whole part of space turns into a free-fire zone! Mr. Chekov, phasers!"

"Ready, Captain," Chekov said. But past *Ortisei,* Jim could see *Saheh'lill* and *Greave* curving around again past *Mascrar,* firing at *Bloodwing* as she passed . . .

. . . and *Saheh'lill*'s phasers hit *Speedwell. Speedwell*'s shields took the fire and held. She flung herself away from the Romulan vessel, forbearing to fire even though orders would have permitted it. *Saheh'lill* curved back toward *Mascrar,* low over the city's surface, very low, still firing, trying to reach *Bloodwing* while she was at close range.

A terrible lance of fire suddenly blasted out from *Mascrar* and struck *Saheh'lill* full on. The Romulan ship simply vanished in it, together with its explosion, its only remnant a long lingering streak of excited ions in the space through which the beam had struck.

Sulu threw *Enterprise* past *Mascrar* in *Bloodwing*'s wake, and the view on the main screen gyred and pinwheeled wildly as Sulu rolled the ship hard on her longitudinal axis, and then up and over in a variant of the ancient Immelmann. Chekov pounced on his console, and then did it again, and two of the torpedoes following *Bloodwing* blew up, small bright clouds of expanding fire in the night. But another one, corkscrewing in pursuit as she did, missed *Bloodwing* as she suddenly straightened and ran straight at *Greave,* firing. *Hheirant,* now plunging away from *Mascrar* and toward *Enterprise,* took the torpedo on her shields. They flickered, went down; she started losing acceleration, limped away.

"How many of those things left?" Jim said.

"Two, Captain. Still tracking *Bloodwing*. She's coming around tight to try to deal with them."

Close by, *Sempach* was closing with the damaged *Hheirant*. "*Hheirant*," Jim heard the comms officer aboard *Sempach* hailing them, "do you have casualties, can we assist—"

Hheirant fired on *Sempach*.

The flagship took the fire on her shields. A long moment's pause . . .

Pillion dived in from the other side and began to fire on *Sempach* as well, while *Hheirant* continued firing.

Sempach yawed hard forward, quickly as a coin being flipped, and her phasers lanced out repeatedly at *Pillion* en passant. *Pillion*'s shields went down under the onslaught, and after a moment she broke off attack and fled out of range. *Hheirant*, though, could not do the same, and as the phasers raked her, she blew.

Once again *Enterprise* and the other ships shuddered and wallowed in the shockwave of the detonation. It passed, and people let go of whatever they had been using to brace themselves and stared at the screen.

Gorget was fleeing, plunging away from RV Trianguli out into the darkness; she cloaked herself and vanished. *Pillion* streaked off in her wake and a second later was also gone.

Bloodwing went after, vanishing as well.

The bridge went very quiet.

"They are all headed toward the Neutral Zone," Spock said. "Projected courses appear to indicate the first two vessels are headed for the Eisn system."

Diane Duane

"Back to ch'Rihan," Jim said softly. "So much for diplomacy. Status of the other ships?"

"*Sempach* has some structural damage, but it does not seem severe. *Ortisei* has no power and has lost pressure in much of her secondary hull; she has been almost entirely evacuated except for a skeleton engineering crew who are trying to stabilize her warp core. *Lake Champlain* is nowhere to be found, though a debris cloud nearby strongly implies that she was destroyed during the engagement. *Hemalat*'s primary hull seems to have taken a hit from a torpedo; she has no warp capacity. Estimated time of repair thirty-six hours. *Nimrod* is not reporting, probably due to communications problems—her readings are otherwise normal. *Speedwell* is reporting that her shield generators took damage during the attack, and shields cannot be raised."

"*Enterprise!*"

It was Danilov's voice. "On screen," Jim said.

Danilov was sitting there in a bridge full of smoke, flickering fire, and outcries. "Captain Kirk," he said, "you are ordered to pursue *Bloodwing* and bring her back to Federation space."

"That may prove difficult, Commodore."

"*Do it,*" Danilov said. "You know what you stand to lose if you don't."

Jim had a pretty good idea. "One thing, Commodore. What is the Federation's stance as regards the commander's request for asylum?"

"They granted it."

Jim raised his eyebrows. "Probably just as well

202

we never had a chance to tell the Romulans so," he said. "A fight could have broken out."

Danilov looked grim.

"As regards *Bloodwing,* Commodore," Jim said, "what if her commander declines to cooperate?"

"Then you are to return to RV Trianguli immediately for debriefing and reassignment."

There were about thirty things that could mean. "Yes, sir," Jim said.

"You are to state that you understand my orders and will comply with them fully and without reservation."

The silence got long. Then Jim turned around to look at Uhura. "What happened to the signal, Lieutenant?" he said.

They exchanged a long look. After a second, she glanced down at her console. She didn't do anything that Jim could see, but she said, "We seem to have lost it, Captain."

When she looked up at him again, her expression was too neutral to read.

"Thank you, Lieutenant," Jim said. "That will be all for the moment." He turned away, looking at Spock.

"Captain . . ." Spock said.

"Mr. Spock," Jim said, "I will want to see you in my quarters briefly in about half an hour. Mr. Sulu, set a course matching *Bloodwing*'s. Pursue her, at warp nine. If you need more speed to catch her, use it. Estimated time to intercept?"

"Twenty minutes, Captain, if we're on the right course. She may have altered."

"Make that an hour from now in my quarters, Mr.

Spock. Uhura, hail her, and at the very least get a course update from her if she's not willing to de-cloak. Sickbay!"

Sickbay had been in turmoil when McCoy got there. The place was full of security personnel who were holding phasers on three people, all on diagnostic beds now. Lia was working busily over one of the two prone forms, getting the scrub field set over him. Another nurse, big, broad-shouldered, mustached Tom Krejci, was tending to the second patient, a young man sitting up in bed and holding a sterile pad over a disruptor wound on his head. *Only a graze,* McCoy thought, for anything better targeted would have burst the young man's head like a rock dropped on a melon. "Put those things down," McCoy said to the security people, "I know this boy, this is tr'AAnikh. He's all right. Tom, what did you give him?"

"Ten mils of orienthrin for the shock, and fifty mikes of entrivate-B for pain relief."

"Give him another five of orienthrin, to be on the safe side." McCoy lifted the sterile pad, looked quickly under it. "Then get busy regenerating that; shouldn't take you more than five minutes. Make sure you keep that protoplaser set below three—Romulan dermal perfusion's a little more leisurely than ours."

"Right, Doctor."

"Okay, son," McCoy said to tr'AAnikh, replacing the sterile pad, "you just hold that there a couple minutes more. Here, have some ale."

Tr'AAnikh sat looking in astonishment at the bottle McCoy had shoved at him as the doctor moved over past the second diagnostic bed. The figure lying there was half draped under a silvery heatcon blanket. Without turning away from the sterile field she was working under, Lia said, "I'm sorry, Doctor. He was already gone when they brought him in. Massive internal disruptor injuries."

McCoy nodded, pulled the blanket up to cover the face, then turned to look over Lia's shoulder at the occupant of the third bed. "He'll be ready for you in about two minutes," she said, her attention focused on the hologram of the patient's organs that had formed under the sterile field cowl. "Nearly stable enough to start work. Dr. M'Benga's on his way."

"Good." McCoy pulled off his duty tunic, chucked it into a nearby clean-or-recycle chute and turned back to the diagnostic bed where tr'AAnikh was sitting. "How'd you get over here in the first place?" McCoy asked, taking the high-sleeved surgical tunic that Krejci handed him and pulling it on. "I don't imagine they let you just waltz in and beam out of there without any authorization."

"The senator helped us," tr'AAnikh said. "Senator Arrhae i-Khellian. She gave us a device that let us get to the infirmary on *Gorget* and get the praetor out without the alarm being raised. Then Hhil and I went to the transporter room with the praetor. The guards there tried to stop us . . ." He looked sorrowfully at the blanket-shrouded form on the next bed.

"They failed," McCoy said, hurriedly sealing up the surgical tunic, "and I suspect that's going to be worth something shortly. But I'm truly sorry about your friend."

"He knew this might happen, and he was prepared for it," tr'AAnikh said. "He and I both wanted to help the commander, and the captain . . . and the senator said this was the best way to do it."

"I hope she's right," McCoy said. "You lie back and rest now." He turned back to Burke. "Lia, is he ready?"

"All set, Doctor. Recorders are running. Field's on invasive visual."

"Right. What have we got?"

Under the sterile field's archlike canopy, and over the patient's ravaged chest, a holographic representation of the contents now superimposed itself, the tissues of the various organs and systems differentiated by shade and intensity of color. Shadowy forms of organs missing or damaged overlaid themselves on the originals. Right now the respiratory and cardiac systems were outlined and highlighted in strident red, indicating both massive trauma and failure status, and showing some big initial forcefield bypasses that Burke had installed to keep the vascular flow going around the patient's heart. "Extensive dorsal supradermal and infradermal burns," Burke said. "I've been infusing adjusted saline by inguinal veinpak to compensate. Extensive crenation of superficial muscular and fascial tissue secondary to disruptor damage. I've debrided the blasted tissue, saved some noncrenated tissue for cloning—it's in the hopper now and first divisions are ongoing. The rest can wait. A lot of intestinal damage, but nothing serious once he's stable: no major bleeding, and I stopped the leakage from the mesentery. The big problem's the heart, as you can see. Someone over there's a good shot."

"Too damn good," McCoy said, looking at the holographic image of the heart. It was a mess, already once partially exploded by disruptor fire, and roughly patched by the Romulan surgeons—they had merely butted the tears in the ventricles together with mechanical crimps and sealed them with inorganic adhesives, and the patching was rapidly coming undone without any replacement connective tissue to keep it in place. *Give them the benefit of the doubt—they may have planned surgery later.* But now the heart had a new set of tears in it from the attack that had just happened. *So. Save or replace?* "Mmm. Primary-degree disruption involvement to upper simulpericardium, anterior atrium, superior diaphragmatic stosis, secondary-degree damage to centricardium, upper right ventricle, upper left ventricle, medial upper ventricular septum." *And look at it, they left all this exploded cellular material in place at the edges.* That *would never have healed. I know* they can do better than this! Did someone over there not want him to survive? Well, tough luck.

"The AV and periHV rhythms in the heart muscle have gone sporadic," Burke said. "They're full of transient conduction spikes due to enzyme flooding, and the new tears are pulling the old ones open. It won't hold long; it's going to rip itself apart again, if it doesn't stop first."

"Damn," McCoy said softly. "Patching this is going

to be a nightmare. Still, we can't risk an artificial heart under the circumstances." Especially since, if things got lively out there and the ship lost power while maneuvering, a heart made of nothing but forcefields would do the praetor no good at all. "Let's rebuild this on the double, and get a spare growing." McCoy poked a spot with the guide protoplaser. "There's the AV node. Lia, harvest me some tissue from there. And for God's sake don't let it stop contracting! I don't want to have to waste time jump-starting it later—"

From the nearby instrument tray, Burke picked up what McCoy routinely referred to as the "magic wand," a foot-long chromed instrument that liaised with the pattern buffer of the surgical transporter under the diagnostic bed. She slipped the wand into the hologram, focused the harvesting field into it in the form of a little sphere of yellow light, used the control on the side of the wand to enlarge the sphere a little, then tightened the sphere's volume down again. "That enough?"

"Hell, take the whole thing. It's not doing him any good at the moment."

The sphere sparkled with transporter effect and vanished, taking the tissue with it into the waiting container of growth medium. "Tom?" Burke said.

"I'll take care of it."

"Sickbay!" said Jim's voice out of the air.

"McCoy here."

"Report, Bones."

She's right, it won't hold, McCoy thought as he spotted the aneurysm forming in the equivalent to the vena cava, swelling out and out like a blown balloon. *Oh no, you don't!* Sweat burst out on his forehead as he grabbed the "guide" protoplaser that Lia handed him, set it for "vascular" and "designate," and swiftly traced a glowing path through the hologram from about two centimeters above the aneurysm to about three centimeters below it. The surgical support system built into the sterile field cowl immediately emplaced a small tubular forcefield into that spot inside the patient, and "marked" it in glowing red for reference. Just as the forcefield patch snugged down and mated to the vessel at the cellular level, the aneurysm blew like a badly patched tire, dark green blood flooding the forcefield segment and turning it brownblack. *Lord, that was close.*

He swallowed, his mouth briefly too dry to speak. "Three people down here, Jim. One dead. One alive and known to me, not seriously injured. One in pretty bad shape—that's the praetor, Jim. Big hole in his gut. Heart's all ripped up. But we're in luck," McCoy added, glancing at one of the readouts in the visualization hologram. "He's a pretty regulation T-positive. I was wondering whether some fraction changes had crept into Romulan serology over time, but it seems not . . ."

"Aren't the T-types rare?" Jim said.

The door hissed as M'Benga came hurrying in, took in the scene at a glance, and immediately started pulling off his duty tunic. "Relatively speaking," McCoy said. "But we'll be OK for a while. I have enough synthetic cuproplasm from the reserve

Diane Duane

stock we keep down here for Mr. Spock to keep Gurrhim's plasma balance acceptable, while we clone the extra fractions needed from the samples Ambassador Sarek left us. M'Benga, you sterile?"

"Five seconds more."

"Good. I'm playing Little Dutch Boy here at the moment, and there are better things for me to be doing. Come reroute these damn bleeders before one of them blows sky high the way the cava just tried to. Every vessel in here's been weakened by the disruptor blast, and we're going to have to fuse in physical replacements for all the majors in the next five minutes." M'Benga slipped in opposite him across their patient, next to Burke. "I want you to 'plast the ones I'm force-patching just as soon as I finish each one.

"Spock, would you be willing to go on marrow stimulants for a couple of days if we need some more whole blood?"

"Certainly, Doctor."

"Good. Stop in and see me later. I've got my hands full right now . . ." He slapped the guide protoplaser into Dr. M'Benga's outstretched hand, picked up another one, and started patching another major vein. "Lia, get me eight pieces of ten-by-ten idioplast and slot them into the transporter pad for Dr. M'Benga's protoplaser, and after that, prep eight more. Then stick two units of cuproplasm into the patient to start with, and prepare three more; he's exsanguinating like mad. And beam out that serosanguinous fluid in the peritoneum before he drowns in it!"

"Right. *Tom?*"

210

"Got it. Our other patient's OK, I'll circulate. Here's the cuproplasm. The AV's cloning."

"What did they do to this man besides shoot him?" M'Benga said softly, starting to patch another of the bursting major coronary vessels.

"Precious little," McCoy muttered. "Which may have been their intention. Because, good God, man, I would have thought those people's medicine was a little more sophisticated than *this*. Look at those burns. Is laser cautery and autografting the best they can do? Got to do something about that after we tend to the major organs. Lia, there's another leak in here, he's losing what blood pressure he has, *hurry up!*"

"Plasm's running, Doctor—"

"Start another, and *find that leak!*"

"Bones," Jim's voice said, "will he live?"

"Maybe. Depends on him. I'll let you know. But meanwhile we should be grateful that whoever tried to kill him was in so much of a hurry. Now let me get on with this!" McCoy finished patching another of the vessels attached to the heart.

"That's the other three big vessels idioplasted," M'Benga said. "The fuse is good and tight. Want me to 'plast that one?"

"Yes, and then start regenerating the nerves while I re-butt those tears in the ventricle and weld them," McCoy said, using the protoplaser to mark two torn pieces of tissue and touching the control that would make the pressor function in the manipulation field pull them together. In the holographic image they met, and he drew the protoplaser down the juncture.

Diane Duane

Granular scar tissue grew and spread between them in its wake, welding them together. "Then start re-sealing the simulpericardium. We've got to get this thing going again real quick."

M'Benga was silent for a moment, then swore under his breath. "The nerves aren't responding."

"Goddam alien myelin! Never mind, right now we'll concentrate on the mechanical aspects." He started sealing another tear in the upper left ventricle. "Will you look at the thickness of this heart muscle? Let's hope it's diagnostic of more kinds of strength than one, because it'd be real annoying to lose this man in post-op. Meanwhile, if we patch it right, it may actually hold. Tom, *let's go, we need more idioplast here!"*

"Bloodwing's responded, Captain,". Uhura said. "But just with her course. Mr. Sulu has it now."

"She's accelerated to warp ten, Captain," Sulu said. "Heading deep into Romulan space—what we would call the neighborhood of 450 Arietis."

Jim shook his head. "Warp *ten?* Well, don't lose her, Mr. Sulu. Match it."

"We may ha' no choice but to lose her after a while," Scotty said from engineering. "We canna maintain warp ten forever."

"Warp eleven now, Captain," Sulu said, shaking his head. "Sir, she shouldn't be capable—"

She sure wasn't at 15 Tri, Jim thought. *"Blood-wing!"*

No reply.

"Bloodwing, reply!"

212

Nothing.

Jim's face set hard. "Mr. Spock—"

"Enterprise," Ael's voice said, "apologies for the delay. We had a technical problem. Are you intact?"

"Yes. But others aren't. Ael, where the hell are you going?"

"Not to ch'Rihan, if that is what you thought," Ael said. "I have no interest in chasing *Gorget* and *Pillion* just now, though I confess to interest in the new technology *Pillion* used to attack us. But for now we can safely let them go. Those who attacked us have paid the price. Meanwhile, I have an urgent appointment in the Artaleirh system. What I must know is, are you coming?"

"You'd better believe it," Jim said. "I am not letting you out of my sight. And when you finish whatever it is you have in mind at Artaleirh, you are coming back to Federation space with me ... or else."

"When we are done at Artaleirh, Captain, I will gladly come back with you, if you still insist. And if, by that point, Starfleet does. But for the next sixteen hours, which is the time it will take us to get there at this speed, let us allow the matter to rest. We have trouble enough ahead of us."

"Which is another thing. Scotty, can we *do* sixteen hours at this speed?"

Scotty sounded annoyed. "With adequate warning, aye. And with constant attention. But we'll suffer some failures and burnouts as a result, and we'll need downtime afterwards, a couple of days' worth

Diane Duane

for sure. And are we expected to fight when we get wherever we're going?"

"Of a certainty," Ael said calmly. "There are nine Grand Fleet vessels meeting us there. None of them, I think, are expecting *Enterprise*, but when they see *Bloodwing*, they will certainly be intent on destroying it, and I feel sure they will try to extend the courtesy to you as well."

Scotty was muttering under his breath. Jim could hardly blame him. "I take it, though," Jim said, "that you're expecting help of some kind."

"Yes," Ael said. "This will be a major engagement, and if conducted properly, it may much shorten this war. I rejoice that you will be present, for your appearance will give the Rihannsu fleet as much pause as the presence of all the other ships which will be arrayed against them."

It was flattery of the most outrageous kind. Still, flattery had to contain a kernel of truth in order to work at all. Jim smiled through the anger . . . just a little. "And another thing," Jim said. "Since when can *Bloodwing* maintain this kind of speed? *What the devil have you done to your engines?*"

"Well," Ael said, "since we left home space, Master Engineer tr'Keirianh has been experimenting with a propulsion concept our people came up with a while ago. Grand Fleet had abandoned it as too dangerous an idea and sent it back to the researchers for more work. But you know how engineers are, once a better way of doing something is suggested to them. Tr'Keirianh simply could not let it be, and eventually he found a

214

way to make it work. If one creates a small local singularity and connects it to the warp engines—"

"Oh, no," Jim said softly, and rubbed his forehead gently, where the headache was already starting. Practically in unison with him, "Oh, *no!*" Scotty said, from down in engineering.

"Why?" Ael said. "Have your people had problems with such a thing? It certainly is somewhat experimental, and it will take a good while yet to work all the bugs out of it. The singularity has a tendency to fail without warning. But K's't'lk said—"

"*Uh*-oh," Jim said. *Bugs indeed!*

"What's the matter? K's't'lk says that the design is one which her people have been using for some years. She had a look at what tr'Keirianh had done and changed a couple of connections in his basic design, but that was all."

"He would have worked it out in a month or so anyway, at the rate he was going," K's't'lk said, from down in engineering. "All I had to do was show him the equivalent system in my own ship. He sorted out the details very quickly."

"Ael," Jim said, "why didn't you tell me you had this?"

"Because for a good while it refused to work except intermittently," Ael said. "When we tried to use it at 15 Trianguli, it failed us when we greatly needed it. But today, at least, it is working. How much better it might work yet remains to be seen. Theoretically it could be pushed as high as warp thirteen. Maybe even more. For the meantime, though, we will hold it at ten, so that you can keep up."

Jim raised his eyebrows. "Nice of you, Commander. I have a few things to deal with here. Would you excuse me for a little while?"

"Certainly, Captain. *Bloodwing* out."

He stood up from the center seat and rubbed his face for a moment. "Mr. Sulu," he said, "if she does anything sudden, I want to know immediately."

"Yes, sir."

He turned to look at Spock. Spock was bent over his scanner again.

"Spock," Jim said, "what is it now?"

"Captain, I am once again picking up that peculiar waveform we detected earlier."

"*What?* Don't tell me another cloaked Romulan ship is on our tail."

Spock straightened, looking surprised. "Not at all, Captain. The waveform is presently coming from sickbay."

Jim's eyes widened, and he headed straight for the turbolift. "Mr. Sulu, you have the conn. Come on, Spock, let's see what gives. Then you and I need to go down to my quarters."

An hour later they were still there, and Jim was just putting a data solid away in the little safe near his desk. Spock stood to one side, turning over and over in his hands the little green metal sphere that the young Rihannsu officer tr'AAnikh had handed over to them.

"So you see my problem," Jim said softly to

Spock as he touched the buttons to reprogram the combination and lock the safe.

"Yes, Captain," Spock said. "It is considerable."

"I'll be informing McCoy about this as soon as he's out of surgery," Jim said. "But I'm afraid the orders don't permit me to confide in the crew . . . at least not yet. We may have problems."

"It is always difficult to predict the future with any accuracy," Spock said, "but I suggest that you may be overestimating the severity of this problem."

"I just hope you're right. Meantime . . ." He looked at the little sphere. "What can you make of that?"

"I believe it will prove very useful," Spock said. "Further analysis will reveal whether its technology can be exploited on a larger scale. If, as I think—"

The intercom whistled. Jim hit the control on his desk. "Kirk here."

"A message has come in from Starfleet Command, Captain, via relay from RV Trianguli."

"Yes?"

"It's Code One, sir."

Jim swallowed.

"I'll be right up."

On *Bloodwing*'s bridge, everything was very quiet. Ael sat there with only tr'Hrienteh for company, looking out as the stars poured past them in the darkness.

"It is," tr'Hrienteh said, "a normal physiological reaction to the stress of battle, Ael. You know that."

"Of course I know it," Ael said. "But surely it is folly to reject sorrow simply because one has just had a victory." She sighed. "Such as it is. What of poor *Lake Champlain,* then? Its crewmen did not think to die on this mission. And as for those who sought, however indirectly, to protect us: this is a sad repayment of their wish to do us justice. Yet at the same time, our own people broke their own truce at the first second they could . . . and if one will deal with such folk, well, that has its dangers. If the Federation was not clear about that before, they are now."

She looked grimly out at the stars. But the grimness could not hold: the sorrow came back to replace it.

Tr'Hrienteh shook her head. "There is no harm in second thoughts, *khre'Riov.*"

"As long as I do not act on them," Ael said. "I have chosen this path. To turn from it because of pity for blood shed now will make that bloodshed worthless. I must go all the way through, for their sakes, for the sake of all those who will shortly die; else it means nothing."

She stood up. "Ask the crew to assemble in the workout room," she said. "This will only take a few minutes. But there may not be time when we reach Artaleirh."

Jim and Spock stood looking over Uhura's shoulder at the screen, where the text version of the message was scrolling. Its detail filled the whole screen, but one part of it mattered most.

. . . previous attacks on Federation vessels and incursions into Federation space. Negotia-

tions regarding these incursions have failed, and
have been followed by a new incursion of a Romulan task force into the space near 15 Trianguli.
These hostile actions have left us no alternative
but to declare that as of this date, a state of war
exists between the United Federation of Planets
and the Romulan Star Empire.

Jim's mouth was dry. "I hoped we would never have
to see this again," he said softly. It had been the Klingons the last time Code One came through, and there
had been more than enough deaths in that awful time,
enough destruction and terror, before the Organians
had abruptly brought that war to a close. This time,
though, they showed no sign of interfering. Jim wondered one more time whether this meant the Organians
were either gone or merely bored with dealing with
lesser races, or whether humans and Romulans did not
have the kind of joint future—bizarre as it sounded
right now—which they had predicted that Klingons
and humans would someday have. *I think we're on our
own this time,* he thought. *But will we have the sense
to end it as quickly as we can, or will we all get stuck
again in the old habit of killing 'aliens' for fun?*
There was no way to tell. The only thing that was
certain was that the Second Romulan War had begun.

In the workout room, with its hung-up floor mats
and its floor scuffed and scarred from thousands of
games and bouts, all of Ael's little crew were waiting for her when she came in. They stared at her, for

she was, for the first time, not in uniform. She was dressed all in pale silver-gray—breeches, tunic, boots—like one going to a wedding or a funeral, and in her hand she held the Sword.

She slipped it out of the scabbard and glanced at Aidoann, who stood off to one side. The blade glinted in the hard light of the room as she tossed the scabbard to Aidoann. Her second-in-command caught it.

"Too long this mighty heirloom has lain hidden," Ael said. "But, for life or death, it will do so no more. I will not sheathe it again until we are done, or our work is done. Ships the Imperium has spent, lives they have spent, and what little honor they had left they have spent hunting the Sword. Now the Sword shall come hunting them. Let us see how well they like it."

The cheer from them nearly deafened her as Ael left the workout room and made her way back up to the bridge. There she laid the Sword naked over the arms of her command seat, and stood behind it a moment, looking out at the main viewscreen's image of the stars.

Then Ael went out, and the Sword lay alone in the stillness and the starlight, with the cold, still, blue-shifted fires streaking and glittering on its blade.

To be continued . . .

Look for STAR TREK fiction from Pocket Books

Star Trek®: The Original Series

Star Trek: The Next Generation®

Star Trek®: Day of Honor

#1 • *Ancient Blood* • Diane Carey
#2 • *Armageddon Sky* • L.A. Graf
#3 • *Her Klingon Soul* • Michael Jan Friedman
#4 • *Treaty's Law* • Dean Wesley Smith & Kristine Kathryn Rusch
The Television Episode • Michael Jan Friedman
Day of Honor Omnibus • various

Star Trek®: The Captain's Table

#1 • *War Dragons* • L.A. Graf
#2 • *Dujonian's Hoard* • Michael Jan Friedman
#3 • *The Mist* • Dean Wesley Smith & Kristine Kathryn Rusch
#4 • *Fire Ship* • Diane Carey
#5 • *Once Burned* • Peter David
#6 • *Where Sea Meets Sky* • Jerry Oltion
The Captain's Table Omnibus • various

Star Trek®: The Dominion War

#1 • *Behind Enemy Lines* • John Vornholt
#2 • *Call to Arms...* • Diane Carey
#3 • *Tunnel Through the Stars* • John Vornholt
#4 • *...Sacrifice of Angels* • Diane Carey

Star Trek®: The Badlands

#1 • Susan Wright
#2 • Susan Wright

Star Trek® Books available in Trade Paperback

Omnibus Editions
    Invasion! Omnibus • various
    Day of Honor Omnibus • various
    The Captain's Table Omnibus • various
    Star Trek: Odyssey • William Shatner with Judith and Garfield
    Reeves-Stevens

Other Books

STAR TREK
THE EXPERIENCE
LAS VEGAS HILTON

Be a part of the most exciting deep space adventure in the galaxy as you beam aboard the U.S.S. Enterprise. Explore the evolution of *Star Trek®* from television to movies in the "History of the Future Museum," the planet's largest collection of authentic Star Trek memorabilia. Then, visit distant galaxies on the "Voyage Through Space." This 22-minute action packed adventure will capture your senses with the latest in motion simulator technology. After your mission, shop in the Deep Space Nine Promenade and enjoy 24th Century cuisine in Quark's Bar & Restaurant.

- -